Vampire's Thirst

ALSO BY CYNTHIA GARNER

Vampire's Thirst

Book 2 of The Awakening Series

CYNTHIA GARNER

FOREVER
YOURS

New York Boston

Copyright © 2014 by Cindy Somerville

Excerpt from *Vampire's Hunger* copyright © 2014 by Cindy Somerville

Cover design by Elizabeth Turner

Cover photography by Claudio Marinesco

Cover lettering by Jen Massuri

Cover copyright © 2014 by Hachette Book Group, Inc.

Forever Yours

Hachette Book Group

237 Park Avenue, New York, NY 10017

Hachettebookgroup.com

Twitter.com/foreverromance

First published as an ebook and as a print on demand edition: May 2014

Forever Yours is an imprint of Grand Central Publishing.

The Forever Yours name and logo are trademarks of Hachette Book Group, Inc.

The publisher is not responsible for websites (or their content) that are not owned by the publisher.

The Hachette Speakers Bureau provides a wide range of authors for speaking events. To find out more, go to www.hachettespeakersbureau.com or call (866) 376-6591.

ISBN 978-1-4555-7923-5 (ebook edition)

ISBN 978-1-4555-5260-3 (print on demand edition)

Acknowledgments

To my readers: Thank you for giving me your support and encouragement. It makes the work that much more worthwhile.

To my agent, Susan Ginsburg: I wouldn't be here without your guidance. Thank you!

To my Grand Central team: From titles to artwork, from revisions to editing, you make my work shine, and I appreciate it. To my editor, Latoya Smith: Your skills always elevate my writing. Thank you for working so hard for me.

To my family: I love you. Thank you for supporting me.

Finally, to my awesome critique partners Suzanne, Roz, and Laura: You always make me stop and take another look, and it makes my stories better. You gals rock!

Vampire's Thirst

Chapter One

Kimberly Treat shoved her back against the rough brick of the building and watched the vampire scout move cautiously forward. She stayed behind with the rest of the group, all vamps except for her. They were on yet another food run, each time having to go farther away from the safety of the compound she now called home. This trip through zombie town had taken them fifteen miles south, and all they had to show for it was one measly bag of canned goods, mostly beans and corn. It wasn't nearly enough for the number of humans living in the enclave. But soon it would be time to plant crops in the space they'd cleared in the courtyard of the complex, and that would help. An ongoing source of protein was still needed, but she could only solve one problem at a time.

The scout came back. Voice low, he said, "There are at least thirty zombies between us and our target."

The target being a grocery store. Chances were slim that they'd find anything, but they had to look.

The scout added, "They seem pretty broken down. I think the six of us can take them."

Six against thirty. The only thing that evened things out was that five in her group were vampires. They had the strength, agility, and speed to stay out of reach of the zombies even while moving in for the kill. But still, there were thirty hungry zombies…

"Ms. Treat, I don't suppose it'd do any good to ask you to wait for us to clear 'em out," Leon, one of the vamps routinely assigned to ensure her safety, murmured in her ear. "Duncan didn't want you to go out in the first place. I don't want to go back and tell him you've been injured. Or worse."

"Yes, well, just because he loves me doesn't mean he gets to tell me what to do." She ignored Leon's muttered comment that Duncan was the leader and she was supposed to do what he said. She shot him a glance from the corner of her eye. Pulling her hatchet free from her belt, she said, "Let's go. The sooner we do this, the sooner we can go home."

"You heard her." Leon jerked his head toward the store. "Let's get moving."

Within seconds they were wading through the horde. Kimber swung her hatchet, catching a zombie in the middle of his forehead. As the body dropped to the ground, she pulled the blade free and moved on to the next one. And the next one. And the one after that.

The vampires with her fought almost silently, with only grunts of exertion coming from them as they swung their weapons. "Leon, behind you!" she heard one of them exclaim.

Kimber twisted in time to see Leon lop off the head of a zombie. Fingers on her shoulder made her swing around to fend off another shuffler. Just as she dispatched him, she heard a cry of pain from behind her. She whirled around to see one of the vampires being pushed to the ground by a couple of zombies.

She shouted and leaped toward them. Even as she moved, she knew she was too slow. Swinging her hatchet at the back of a rotting head, she was too weak to make a significant impact. Teeth began ripping and chewing vampire flesh, confirming her attack on the zombie was futile.

"No!" She brought her hatchet down again.

"Ms. Treat." Leon yanked her back, shoving her into the arms of another vampire just as a shuffler reached out for her. "Get to the store," he ordered.

"Not without you." Kimber struggled to get free. "Leon!"

"I'll be right behind you." He swung his sword and lopped off the heads of two zombies. "I can't leave Darron like this."

Kimber and the remaining vampires headed toward the store. She glanced over her shoulder and watched as Leon brought his sword down and decapitated the downed vampire. Now the zombies could use his body as food, but he would be in no danger of turning.

While vampires' ability to heal themselves was remarkable, with the kind of damage he'd already suffered, his powers of regeneration couldn't have kept up with the spread of the tainted Unseen, the mystical force that had once helped her reanimate corpses in her job as a necromancer—and that very possibly had, through her, started the zombie apocalypse.

If not stopped here and now, Darron would become a zombie, one with the strength and speed of a vampire. They couldn't allow that to happen, which was why vampires fought with man-made weapons instead of their teeth.

Kimber reached the store and turned around, waiting for Leon. He sprinted toward them, his bloody sword whirling, stabbing as he fought his way past the few remaining zombies. His face grim, he said, "Let's go inside. We need to gather whatever provisions we can find and get the hell out of here."

Twenty minutes later, they were on their way with several large bags filled with foodstuffs. There wasn't a lot but they had enough to feed the dozens of humans at the compound for several weeks on a rationed basis. It wasn't until they passed through the gates of the enclave that Kimber relaxed. She mourned for the loss of Darron but knew there was nothing anyone could have done to save him. From the minute the first zombie began biting him, his life had been over. Because of his sacrifice, others would continue to live.

* * *

Duncan MacDonnough scrubbed his hand over his chin and stared at his second-in-command. Frustration and irritation made his eyes burn and his fangs elongate. "I don't need this right now, Atticus." He tried his best to look stern but feared he came across as whiningly imploring. Not the impression a newly minted leader of vampires should make. "Tell me you're not serious."

"Sorry, no can do. I am serious." Marcus Atticus shrugged broad shoulders and slouched down into one of two plush, dark brown leather armchairs in front of Duncan's wide mahogany desk. The desk faced the large windows in what had been the former queen's throne room but now served as Duncan's office.

The vampire enclave was housed in one of the multistory buildings of a refurbished tire factory in Akron, Ohio. While the outside of the building remained the same from Maddalene's long and autocratic rule, the inside had seen some changes, not the first of which was the room where Duncan and Atticus now sat.

The plush chaise the queen had used to lounge on, along with her beefy human consorts, was gone. And good riddance. Duncan still bore some scars on his back from the whipping Maddalene had given him, chained to the central post in the middle of the room, over his choosing to be loyal to his human lover instead of his vampire queen. The marks weren't as bad as she'd meant them to be only because he'd been able to feed soon after the beating.

But still, yeah. Good riddance. To more than the damned chaise.

Atticus tapped his fingers on the wide arm of his chair. "Most of the humans who have signed up to live here as…donors…are fine with staying with the vamps they're assigned to. But a few have decided it's too dangerous—they're afraid their chosen benefactors will be more likely to lose control if their food source is too close, so instead they want to stay within the area we've assigned to new human arrivals."

"I don't have an issue with that." Duncan's hold on his already strained patience began to unravel, and he forced himself to remain calm. This was Atticus, his best friend and someone he knew would always look out for him. He didn't deserve having Duncan take out his frustrations on him. "Why are you acting like it's a problem?" Duncan asked.

"Because they're inciting unrest. Most of them are fine. They understand the danger on the outside. But there are a few who say they don't like being cooped up, unable to leave the compound. They feel like prisoners." The other vampire scowled. "They want to go to the park. Can you believe that?"

Duncan stared at Atticus. There were times when he just didn't get humans—and lately those times were coming more and more. "The closest one is Glendale Park, which is at least a mile and a half away. Don't they understand that if they leave the compound, they risk being overrun by zombies?" He rubbed a hand over his face. "Is a walk in the park worth it?"

The other vampire lifted one shoulder in a nonchalant shrug. "They want a vampire escort for protection."

Duncan snorted. Was this what his life had been reduced to? Listening to petty gripes all day long? No wonder Maddalene had been such a bitch. "They can want all they like. I'm not risking anyone unnecessarily just because humans with cabin fever want to take a stroll." He gestured toward the wide window that faced a courtyard between buildings. They'd established a sturdy fence around the courtyard and had vamps on guard 24/7. "They can walk there."

"They say it's not the same."

"Well, I suppose a mile-and-a-half zombie run would give them plenty of exercise." Duncan grinned. "Hmm. Maybe I should rethink this."

Atticus gave a snort. "Don't encourage them." He paused, another scowl turning down his mouth. "One of them punched Natalie in the face this morning."

"What?" Duncan surged to his feet. Natalie Lafontaine was the best friend of his lover Kimber Treat, and over the last several months, she had become his friend as well. While he had a duty to keep the humans in his care secure, he was especially committed to keeping Kimber and Natalie safe. That Natalie, acting as a liaison between humans and vampires, would be in jeopardy and attacked by her own kind was a possibility that had never entered his mind. "What the hell! We're giving them sanctuary from zombie hordes," he said, bringing up his hands to tick off a list on his fingers. "We keep them safe, we feed them, we clothe them, and all we ask in return is that they provide nourishment once a week to one vampire only. The amount of blood they give isn't even a quarter of what they'd donate to a blood bank."

"I know, but they're afraid." Atticus hunched forward to clasp his hands between his knees. "Natalie tries to allay their fears, but they don't seem to want to listen." He shook his head. "I get that they're scared of us. We're predators, every last one of us. But we provide safety they have little chance of having outside this compound."

Duncan rubbed the back of his neck and dropped into his chair. "Fuck a goddamn duck, Atticus. When we overthrew

Maddalene a month ago, I would never have envisioned the
kind of difficulties we're having with humans. I thought killing
Maddalene was the hard part. Unlike her, who viewed humans
as things to be used and discarded, we treat them with dignity
and provide them a safe haven from the hordes. We're still rebuilding trust—not just between humans and vampires, but
from one vampire to another." He sent a frown his friend's way.
"I have enough on my plate keeping our people in line. I don't
have time to deal with trouble-making humans, too. That's why
I have you. Deal with it."

"That was the plan all along. I already took care of the son
of a bitch who hit Nat. He won't be breathing through his nose
for a while. Or taking nourishment except through a straw."
Another nonchalant shrug lifted one wide shoulder. "I just
wanted to keep you in the loop." He cleared his throat. "So, have
things with you and Kimber settled down?"

Duncan shot him a glare. "There was nothing to settle down.
We're fine." He did his best to believe it, but his friend was a very
discerning man.

"Uh-huh." Atticus cocked his head to one side, his silver eyes
missing nothing.

Damn him. The former Roman gladiator was over 2,000
years old, not that he'd ever given Duncan an exact birth date.
Maybe he was so old he didn't remember. It happened sometimes.

Those silver vampire eyes narrowed on him now. "She's acting
like she's in perpetual PMS, my friend. Something isn't right,
and don't try to tell me otherwise."

Duncan fought the flinch that wanted to work its way over his face. Kimber had been getting more and more aggressive, and he couldn't help but think the reason was that small amount of the Unseen that had lodged in her soul. He was worried that the Unseen was tainted and would somehow overtake her innate goodness. But what kind of leader would he be if he let that worry show, even to his most trusted friend?

Duncan folded his arms across his chest. "Oh, for fuck's sake, Atticus. Just what the hell would you know about PMS, anyway?"

"I know about women," came the smug reply.

Duncan couldn't argue with that one. It seemed that all any female, vampire or human, had to do was take one look at Atticus and become mindless with lust. He wasn't sure how much of that was Atticus himself and how much of it was due to his age. The longer a vampire lived, the more powerful he became. And power took on all sorts of forms, including sexual attraction. Atticus had that to spare. If it weren't for having Kimber in his life, Duncan would have been jealous of the other vampire's easy sway over women.

But he had Kimber. For the moment, anyway. Over the last month, while he'd been solidifying his hold over the enclave, he'd sensed her drawing away from him. Emotionally. Physically they were still as attracted as ever, but there was something she held back from him, some part of herself she didn't want him to see. How could they truly be together if she wouldn't confide in him?

The door opened and one of his best warriors, Leon, walked into the room, his blood-spattered face somber.

His gut tight with dread, Duncan sprang to his feet. "Kimber?"

"Miss Treat is fine. Not a scratch. She's planning on coming to see you once she gets cleaned up." Leon raked one hand through his hair. "We lost Darron."

Even while relief spiraled through him that Kimber was all right, anger and grief spread at the loss of a good vampire. "Damn it. And these humans expect us to take them to the park safely when we can't even scavenge for food without losing one of us?" Duncan shared a grim look with Atticus before turning his attention back to Leon. "Were you able to get more food?"

"Yes. Miss Treat estimates they have enough for maybe two months as long as they stay on rationed portions."

Duncan sank back into his chair. "Thank you, Leon. Go get cleaned up."

"Yes, sir."

Duncan waited until the door closed before he pushed out a sigh. "One step forward, two steps back. That's our dance, isn't it?" He clenched his fists on top of his desk. "Damn her. I don't want Kimber going out and risking herself this way."

"She feels she must contribute." Atticus lifted one shoulder. "She wouldn't be the woman you love if she didn't."

He was right, of course. Damn.

Atticus pushed to his feet, drawing Duncan's attention. "I'm going to check on Natalie," his second-in-command murmured. "And maybe get a bite to eat while I'm there." He winked, then tipped his head toward the closed door that led into the hallway. "Kimber's coming."

Duncan caught her scent as the door swung open. He shot a glance at his friend. "Keep me posted."

"You bet." Atticus paused beside the redhead standing just inside the doorway and pressed a kiss to her cheek. "Hey there, sweetheart."

"Atticus." She smiled and patted his shoulder. "Nat was looking for you."

"I'm on my way to see her." He closed the door behind him.

Kimber clicked the lock in place and walked toward Duncan.

He stood and moved around to the front of his desk, resting his buttocks on the edge, and watched her move farther into the room. She wore her usual T-shirt and jeans, both garments hugging her slim curves. His body reacted as it always did; his cock began to harden, his fangs elongated, and lust and love burned his eyes.

Her auburn hair fell to her shoulder blades, longer than it had been when this whole mess started, longer than when he'd first met her over a year ago. Her hazel eyes met his and a slow smile curved her full lips.

"I know that look," he said in a low voice, and drew her into a loose embrace. Clasping his hands at the small of her back, he pulled her between his spread legs.

"What look would that be?" She pressed a kiss to his chin, his jaw, just beneath his ear. Her hands lifted, fingers threading through his hair, the light tugs zinging straight to his balls.

A shudder of need worked its way through his body. He took

her mouth with his, deep, hard, a kiss of possession. Of being possessed. Breaking the kiss, he stared into her eyes. "The look that says you want me and mean to do something about it."

"Damn straight. I just survived a food excursion and I need to celebrate being alive." Her smile widened. "I'm here for a nooner." She pressed her lips to the indent at the base of his throat. She undulated against him, her belly slowly grinding against his erection.

"It's one o'clock in the morning," he managed to say on a groan. Until Kimber, no woman had been able to drive his desire so high so fast.

"Well, since you don't usually start work until after dark, and sunset was at eight-thirty, this is your noon."

"I have a one-thirty appointment." He cupped her ass and dragged her fully against him, letting her feel the rigid length of his cock against her belly. She moaned and deepened the kiss, driving her tongue into his mouth, winding it around his own in an ancient dance of pleasure and need. She leaned into him, pressing against the space between his legs, and he pulled her closer.

"This won't take long," she murmured against his lips. She yanked at the waistband of his pants, unbuttoning, unzipping, and getting his pants and underwear around his thighs so his hard cock sprang free. She gripped him, sliding her hand from base to tip and slipping her thumb across the sensitive tip.

He groaned. "Too many clothes," he muttered, fingers working at the button at the waistband of her jeans. He wanted her naked. Now. He shoved her jeans and panties over her hips and pushed them to her ankles. She toed off her shoes, then kicked out of the garments pooled around her feet. With a wiggle and a smile, she drew her shirt over her head, letting it fall to the floor.

Duncan made quick work of getting Kimber out of her bra and stared at her a moment. "God, you're beautiful," he rasped. He leaned forward and swiped his tongue over one of her nipples, then the other, and straightened to see them tighten into hard, puckered nubs. "Sit where I am," he said, his voice rough as he moved to give her his place on the edge of the desk.

She arched a brow but did as he asked, perching on the wooden surface. "Okay, but I'm going to mess up your desk. I'm already wet." She wriggled a bit, trying to get comfortable.

"I hope so." He dragged a chair to where she sat, then even closer, settling between her splayed legs. As he took his place, he looked up at her for a moment, and it was clear she knew his intent. Already her breath came unsteadily as she moved closer to the edge to grant him greater access to the soft folds between her thighs. She leaned back, breasts thrusting up.

With his hands just inside her knees, he spread her legs wider and looked at the pussy before him. She was pink and wet and swollen. *His.* The musk of her desire perfumed the air, that sweetly spiced scent that was uniquely Kimber. He placed his thumbs on the outer lips of her sex and spread her open before he lowered his mouth to taste her. As he lazily traced her with the tip of his tongue, being careful not to nick her with his fangs, she gasped and jolted and gripped at the desktop. He covered her clit for a moment, sucking the sensitive bud of nerves into his mouth, rolling it gently between his teeth. Her gasps and moans grew louder, the sweetest sounds he'd ever heard.

"Duncan!" She bucked up into his mouth, demanding in her need. "Stop fooling around and make me come."

Demands he ignored. He built her pleasure, taking her higher and higher, then backing off, before once more ratcheting up her passion until she fell apart in his arms. He left her clit and languidly licked her slit over and over. As he found a rhythm, stroking her entrance with firm swipes of his tongue, she lifted her hips against him, moaning, and propped up on her elbows.

He focused once more on her abandoned clit, swirling his tongue around the bud first with light pressure, then increasing it bit by bit, swipe by swipe until she was shaking, just on the edge of orgasm.

With a moan of his own, he sucked her hard and pressed two fingers deep into her sheath. She dropped flat on her back, her hips lifting off his desk, a scream of pleasure erupting from her throat that likely was heard throughout the complex. Her hips bucked. He continued his sensual torment even after her butt rested once more against the desk, her breasts rising with her gulping breaths. Only when she was finally still did he push the chair back and stand.

Before he could turn her over to take her from behind, she slid off the desk. "I want you inside me." She put her hands on his shoulders. "Now. I want to ride you."

Even as he wondered anew at her aggression, in this instance he thought it wasn't such a bad thing. He grinned and went down on his knees, then his back. She came down over him, knees on either side of his hips. One slender hand gripped his erection and pointed it where she wanted him. She dropped onto him, taking him deep with one smooth movement. She cried out and bucked with a second orgasm almost immediately. He clasped her hips, holding her where he wanted her, and thrust up, fighting his way in and out of her swollen flesh with no thought beyond wanting to explode with blinding release. The base of his spine tingled and his balls drew up tight against his body. At the moment his orgasm gripped him, his release jetting into her wet heat, he reared up and sank his fangs into the softness of her throat. She jerked and cried out, but as the pain of the bite faded, she gave a low, needy moan.

Her blood tasted rich and sweet. *His*. This incredible woman was his.

Slender fingers clutched at him, nails digging into his shoulders. The slight sting of pain enhanced his passion, and he drank a little deeper. She moaned with pleasure, another climax rocketing through her. When it was done, he licked over her wound and wrapped his arms around her, holding her naked body close, clinging to her. For these few brief moments, his heart beat and his body and mind soared with pleasure so powerful he could do nothing more than shudder against her.

"I love you." Her words were so soft he almost missed them. And that was saying something, since as a vampire he had a heightened sense of hearing.

Keeping his cock firmly embedded in her slick channel, he gently pushed her shoulders back so he could look into her eyes. Sliding his hands from her shoulders, he cupped her face. Her lovely, sweet face. "That's the first time you've said it," he said, and dropped a kiss against the corner of her mouth.

Her eyes were dark, glittering with an emotion he couldn't decipher. It was almost like…anger. Maybe even hate. But he didn't sense those emotions from her. All he felt was affection. And the love she professed.

"You've never said it, either," she said, her voice soft yet still holding a thin thread of steel.

He frowned. "Sure I have."

She shook her head. "No, you haven't. I've been listening very hard for those three words, and you've never said them."

"I've felt them, Kimber." Duncan kissed her, a lingering melding of lips, of hearts. "I do love you. So much."

She wrapped her arms around his waist and hugged him. She yawned, her breasts rubbing against his shirt. After a few minutes she lifted off him, and he let loose a growl of complaint at the sense of loss he felt when his cock left the haven of her body. She gave him a saucy grin and a quick kiss on one corner of his mouth. "You want more, you'll have to come across the hall." She got to her feet and stared down at him, passion written all over her face and in the tense stance of her slender body. "You should come with me now. I want you again."

He wished he could, but his next appointment was important. He shook his head as he stood. He righted his clothing, tucked his cock into his pants, and zipped up. "I have a meeting with Xavier. I can't cancel it."

Annoyance and that ever-present aggression flashed in her eyes, turning the hazel to a vibrant green before she tamped it down with an effort he could see. "I know," she said, her eyes hazel once more. She took a breath, as if fighting for control, and pressed a slender hand to his cheek. "I realize this partnership is important. If we can establish a safe corridor between here and Cleveland, all of us will be more secure and better able to get supplies."

He helped her get dressed, though it took longer than it would have if she'd been on her own. Every few seconds he had to pause to stroke and kiss. When she was finally clothed, she seemed to have her emotions under control. With a teasing expression, she clucked her tongue and stared at him. "You didn't even take off any of your clothes."

He grinned. "That's the advantage men have, I suppose."

She rolled her eyes. "Well, when you decide to come to bed, you may find that advantage won't work for you there." She went on her tiptoes and pressed a soft kiss against his mouth, then moved away. Heading toward the door, she sent him a look over her shoulder that was full of promise. "See you later."

"Count on it."

After she'd gone, Duncan walked back around his desk and sat down. He could feel the grin on his face and knew he probably looked like a lovesick sap, but he didn't care.

She loved him.

Finally, Kimber Treat loved him.

Chapter Two

Kimber retreated to the quarters she shared with Duncan. Giving a nod to the two vampires who guarded their suite, she twisted the knob and pushed open the door. After she closed it behind her, she leaned against it for a moment, rolling her forehead over the cool surface while she tried to fight the aggression that threatened to once again boil over. Eyes scrunched shut, palms pressed hard against the smooth metal surface, she clenched her jaw and drew a deep breath through her nose. Slow exhale. Another breath in. And out. Again.

She would not give in to the swirl of dark energy living inside her. She *couldn't* give in. To give in would admit defeat. Would grant dominance to the Unseen—that shadowy place where all life began and ended, the supernatural realm that she tapped into for the power of necromancy—and she had no intention of doing that. Ever.

She only needed to find a way to get it out of her. That had to be why she was being so aggressive lately. And getting worse every day. Whatever had animated the dead and brought about the apocalypse had left a sliver inside her, a force she hadn't really felt until she'd used her ability to put down some zombies. It had taken a lot out of her and left something behind. Something dark. Something menacing.

Something that wanted to be free, but she sensed it didn't want to rejoin the greater Unseen. No, it wanted to wreak havoc here in the human realm.

And it planned to use her to do it. Whatever *it* was.

She pushed away from the door and collapsed onto the thickly cushioned dark leather sofa in the living room. With a sigh, she toed off her athletic shoes. Leaning her head against the back of the couch, she lifted her legs to rest her heels on top of the glass and chrome coffee table. Duncan's decorating sense was much more sleek and modern than she preferred, and while she had moved in with him, she hadn't gotten around to redecorating anything even though he'd given her permission. There was still plenty of furniture stored in the basement in an area that wasn't needed for any other use at the moment.

She loved him and wanted to believe that he loved her, but she wasn't quite there yet. She just couldn't shut up that soul-sucking inner voice: *If he knew everything that was going on with you, he'd walk away. If he only knew how often you want to reach out and hurt someone for no other reason than that you can, he might not be as enamored with you.*

Oh, sure, he was a vampire and leaned toward violent tendencies himself, but it was something else entirely when your human girlfriend started bitch-slapping people around. When he'd bitten her throat to drink her blood, part of her had wanted to knock him away so *she* could bite *him*. Not for his blood, but for the violence of the act. Then when he'd refused to cancel his appointment with Xavier Vachon, even though she knew it was important, she'd wanted to strike out at him.

What the hell was wrong with her?

A knock at the door sounded. One of the guards, his voice muffled by the closed door, said, "Ms. Treat, Natalie's here to see you."

Kimber sighed. Since she'd put herself on the same schedule as Duncan, she felt like she hardly ever got to be by herself anymore. If she wanted to spend time with her lover, she had to work when he did so they were off together. And since vampires were nocturnal, she'd rearranged her schedule accordingly.

She really wanted to ignore her visitor, but this was her best friend, and she would always make time for Natalie. She got to her feet and went to the door. Pulling it open, she scowled at the guard on her left, a big brute of a man who stood at least six and a half feet tall with a face that looked like it had been on the losing side of one too many fights. "Leon, how many times do I have to tell you to call me Kimber?" she asked.

His only response was a shrug.

Natalie laughed and threw an arm around Kimber's shoulders. "Don't even try, hon. I hooked him up with his donor and he still insists on calling me Ms. Lafontaine." She snickered and sauntered through the door.

"It is a sign of respect," he said, his tone reflecting tolerance at repeating the argument against using their first names. "You are the two highest ranking females here. It would be inappropriate for me to be too familiar with you."

Kimber heaved a sigh and shook her head. "Leon, we kill zombies together. Trust me. Being too familiar with me is *not* when you use my first name. It's when you know the color of my underwear."

A slight flush of pink tinged his chiseled cheeks.

"Dear God, Kimber." Natalie snorted. Her blue eyes twinkled with suppressed humor. "Only you could make a vampire blush."

Taking pity on the uncomfortable guard, she gave him a wink and pushed the door shut. She plopped down on the sofa again and kicked up her feet. "Is this a friendly visit or are we gonna talk shop?"

"Oh, it's a friendly visit for sure, 'cause you're my friend, but we need to talk about work."

"You want coffee or anything?"

Natalie shook her head. "No, I'm good."

"So, how are things working out between you and Atticus?" Kimber watched her friend closely. If she found out the vampire was mistreating her, the bitch-slapping would start with him. And she'd have a reason.

"Okay." When Kimber raised her eyebrows, Natalie grimaced. "We're fine, really. It's just…" She heaved a sigh. "It's only blood. I mean, we aren't, you know." She shifted around on the couch.

"You aren't having sex. Is that what you're trying to tell me in a completely rational, adult way?" Kimber pressed her lips together to hold back a grin.

"Yes." Natalie's arch look dared Kimber to comment further. She spoiled it by laughing. "I can't even imagine having sex with him. Really, he's so intimidating, don't you think?"

"He's sex on a stick," Kimber retorted. "If I weren't with Duncan, I could totally do Atticus."

"'Do' him? Now who's describing sex like an adult?"

Kimber raised her hand with a smirk. "That'd be me." She sobered and folded her arms over her chest. "Seriously, though, how are things between you two?"

"They're fine. Really. I think he'd have sex with me in a heartbeat, so to speak, if I let him know I was interested. But I'm still in love with Aodhán. Until I know for sure that nothing's going to happen with him and me, I can't move forward with Atticus or anyone else. I'd feel like I was cheating." Her full lips turned down in a soft frown.

"It's not like he made any promises." Kimber changed her position, sitting cross-legged to face her friend. "He said goodbye. Not 'see you later,' or 'see you around,' or 'I'll be back, please wait for me.'"

Natalie's sigh held a wealth of heartbreak. "Especially not 'wait for me.'" She gave a sad one-shouldered shrug. "And it's not like he ever told me he loved me. 'Course, I didn't tell him, either. I thought we had more time." Her hard laugh was as brittle as shattered glass. "Wasn't that stupid? We're in the middle of a zombie apocalypse, for cryin' out loud. Either one of us could have died at any time. Me more so than him."

"And he knew that, too, Nat." Kimber leaned forward and took her friend's hands in hers. She tightened her grip around Natalie's cold fingers. "He could have said something." He *should* have said something. Why were men wired to not talk about their feelings? It didn't matter if they were human, vampire, or fey. It was damned frustrating.

"Maybe..." Natalie drew her hands away and wrapped her arms around her waist. "Maybe he didn't love me. Maybe it was just wishful thinking on my part." She blinked fast, clearly trying to stem the tide of tears pooling in her eyes.

Okay, so maybe the bitch-slapping would start with that punk-assed fairy Aodhán the next time she saw him. She loved him like a brother, but the dude was messing with her best friend. "Listen, I'm not going to tell you what to do." She ignored Natalie's mumbled "Since when?" to say, "Only you can decide your future. But think about this: Aodhán's only been gone a month. It's possible he could come back at any time."

"He said he was going to check on his people. That takes a month?"

Kimber spread her hands. "Time moves differently in the fey realm. Slower. It may have only been a day in fey time since he's been gone."

"Really?"

Kimber grimaced at Natalie's hopeful look. "I don't know for sure. He tried to explain it to me once, very scientifically, and my head about exploded. I just know a lot more time has passed here than there."

Natalie heaved another sigh. "Well, I guess even if it's been a month same as here, I owe him more time. I owe *myself* more time. I'd hate to get involved with Atticus and have Aodhán show up." She met Kimber's gaze. "Besides, it wouldn't be fair to Atticus. He's a good guy, even if he is a biter."

Kimber laughed. "You sound like I did a few months ago with my phobia about Duncan biting me."

"Yeah, well, it still makes me a little nervous when I see those fangs coming toward my arm. Still, I don't mind giving him blood directly from the source, not really."

They fell silent, each in their own thoughts, until Natalie said, "Okay, now onto business." She kicked her shoes off and leaned against the arm of the sofa. Pulling her knees up, she loosely clasped her hands in front of her shins, resting her feet on the couch. "We got several new donor recruits in today. I've completed the initial interviews, and for the most part they seem relieved to be here. A little scared, but that's to be expected."

"They'll meet with Atticus tomorrow?"

Natalie nodded. "And probably Duncan as well. They'll want to assure the newcomers that the human living quarters are off-limits to all but a few vampires and that those vamps pose no danger to them."

"Do you have any immediate insights on pairings?"

Her friend tipped her head to one side and pursed her lips. "Maybe. There's a blonde I think would put up with Leon's formality, maybe even get him to loosen up a little." She grinned. "She's feisty."

"Poor Leon." Kimber smiled, and the two of them laughed.

"There's more, and it's really interesting." Natalie paused, chewing on her lower lip.

Kimber raised an eyebrow. "Will we get to the interesting part soon? Or are you on fey time?"

Natalie's lips twitched in a grin. "Two of them say they're necromancers."

Kimber's heart sped up. "Really?" Excited at the thought of having someone else around who was like her, she wanted to go down right away to meet them, talk to them about everything. She paused as another emotion hit her. What if they were *better* than her? God knew they had to be lighter and fluffier than her, what with her holding evil incarnate inside of her. At least it felt that way most of the time. She looked at Natalie. "What did you think of them?" she asked.

Natalie drew in a breath. "I didn't pick up any negative vibes, if that's what you mean. They seemed okay. They want to meet you."

Just like that, Kimber's temper flared. She jumped to her feet with a low-throated growl. "Well, of course they want to meet the renowned Kimber Treat, vampire lover and bringer of apocalypses. Damn it!"

Natalie frowned. "I'm pretty sure they don't think that, Kimber. They weren't disrespectful or mean or anything."

"Well, they wouldn't be to you, would they? You decide if they get to stay or not, more so than me."

"You're the girlfriend of the vampire king, sweetie." Natalie stood, her frown growing deeper. "I think that rank beats mine, which is only friend of the girlfriend of the vampire king."

Make that the *only* friend, and it was a pretty accurate statement. At that realization, Kimber's mad lost its steam. She closed her eyes for a moment. When she looked at Natalie, the other woman still wore an expression of concern, so Kimber hastened to reassure her. "I'm fine, Nat. Just pitching a small hissy, that's all. I'm tired, I guess. It's dark outside and my body thinks I should be sleeping, not running around do-ing…things."

"Things" being her boinking the leader of the vampires while he was supposed to be working. Other than keeping Duncan satisfied in bed, Kimber had no real function here at the compound. Except to try to figure out how to stop the apocalypse. Since it was supernatural in nature and not viral, the zombies kept on coming. As long as people were stupid enough or unlucky enough to get bitten, the hordes continued to increase. Only by pushing the Unseen back into itself would the "contagion" be neutralized.

She hadn't had much luck in doing that. Oh, she'd been able to put down a few zombies, but at such physical risk to herself that Duncan had finally ordered her to stop trying. He seemed fine with the idea that connecting Akron and Cleveland with a protected corridor would be the new reality, and the rest of the world could go to hell.

She just wasn't ready to give up yet.

"Well, there's nothing that says I can't go down and say howdy to the newcomers." She paused and grimaced. "Oh. Do you think they're still up?" At Natalie's shrug, Kimber said, "Well, I'll find out, I guess, when I get down there." As she headed for the door, she glanced at Natalie, who was right be-hind her. "You're coming, too?"

Her friend covered a yawn and shook her head. "Knock your-self out, friend. I'm going to bed." She walked out the door and said, "Oh, their names are Maggie and Jason."

In the hallway the two women headed in opposite directions. Kimber went down to the lobby and headed toward the service stairs that would take her to the basement level where the non-paired humans were housed. As usual, there were vampire guards at that door, too.

"Fellas," she greeted. "I'm going down to meet the newbies, if that's all right."

"Of course," one of them replied. He punched in the code, keeping it hidden with his other hand, and pushed open the door for her.

"Thanks, Al." She gave both guards a jaunty smile and went down the stairs. When she reached the bottom, she looked out over the large open area that served as a common room. Along one wall were a couple of old pinball machines and a foosball table. A Ping-Pong table was nearby, and next to it was a billiard table. Another wall was covered with floor-to-ceiling bookshelves that were crammed with books of every genre, thanks to the Akron-Summit County Public Library system.

At this time of the morning there were only a few people lounging about on several sofas in the room. They looked up at her but didn't say anything. She caught some wariness in their gazes along with a healthy dose of uncertainness. "Hey, welcome. I'm Kimber Treat." She looked around the small group. "I'm looking for Maggie and Jason."

Two people sitting on the couch closest to the corner by the bookshelves stood. "That'd be us," the man said. He put his arm around the woman, and Kimber saw the roundness of her belly. She was pregnant. In the middle of an apocalypse.

She wouldn't want to be her.

"You're the head vamp's mistress, aren't you?" A burly man moved to block her as she headed toward the couple.

She stopped and looked up into his face. This guy wasn't uncertain or afraid. He was pissed off. Well, he'd picked the wrong woman to go all He-Man over. Maybe she'd get some bitch-slapping in today after all.

When she didn't reply, he took a step closer. "Well, are you?"

Now he was in her personal space and starting to piss her off. "You need to back up, my man." It didn't matter that he was at least half a foot taller than her and outweighed her by probably a hundred pounds. If he wanted to go, she'd give him what he was asking for. That bulbous nose of his looked like it needed rearranging.

"Answer the question."

She put one hand on her hip. "Yes, I'm Duncan MacDonnough's girlfriend."

He leaned down and put his face a few inches from hers. "You take him a message for me, missy. Tell him Big Tom demands we be allowed to get out for some fresh air. He can't keep us caged down here." He gestured around with one big hand. "There aren't even any windows."

"Being down here is for your protection," she said, repeating words she knew he'd heard before. "And you are allowed to get fresh air. It's called the courtyard."

He shook his head. "Not good enough. We want to go to the park. Throw a ball around. Play some football. We're going crazy down here." He backed up a few steps and hunched his shoulders. "Look, I'm sorry I got in your space like that. Would you please just talk to him?"

Damn it. No bitch-slapping to be had here, either. She drew a calming breath. "Sure. Look, he's well aware of how you feel. He's just trying to keep you safe without endangering others."

"Right." He shook his head and walked away, grumbling under his breath.

Kimber watched him for a moment, then continued over to the two necromancers. They shook hands in greeting and sat on the sofa while Kimber took a comfy armchair across from them.

"I've been wanting to meet you for a long time," Maggie said. Her voice was soft, her attitude sincere. "Your work before the Outbreak was the stuff of legends."

Kimber stared at her. Uncomfortable with the hero worship she saw in the other woman's eyes, she said, "Uh, thanks."

"Of course, considering many people believe you started the apocalypse, you could probably say your work during the Outbreak was the stuff of legends, too." Jason's tone was as dry as autumn leaves.

"Yeah, thanks for that, too." She shot him a glance.

"I didn't say I believe it," he added with a slight smile.

"Actually..." Maggie looked hesitant, her gaze darting from Kimber to Jason and back again.

"Actually what?" Kimber asked.

"We think we know how it happened. The Outbreak, I mean."

Kimber leaned forward. Her heart thudded a staccato beat behind her ribs. "Tell me."

"I knew a guy, another necromancer from Columbus, who was contacted by the former vampire leader."

"Maddalene Vanderpool," Kimber offered.

Maggie nodded. "Yeah. Anyway, she had this guy come up here to raise her dead lover, only something went wrong. He got a spark but needed more power, so Maddalene slit his throat and let him bleed out over her lover's corpse. I guess she thought the blood would be enough to finish it, but she was wrong." Her lower lip trembled for a moment before she gathered control of her emotions. "The necromancer died and the reanimation was aborted just before completion."

"What does that have to do with the Outbreak?" Kimber asked. "And how do you know all this?"

Maggie swallowed. "I was there." A sad half smile tilted one corner of her mouth. "I was the other necromancer's apprentice." Her gaze locked onto Kimber's. "When did the Lazarus corpse you were dealing with go nuts on you and bite the ME?" she asked.

"The Monday before Thanksgiving, around nine in the evening." Kimber tried to keep her mind from revisiting that awful night but, as usual, couldn't. The man she'd revived in order to find out who'd killed him had brought along a little something extra, and before she could send him back to true death, he'd attacked the medical examiner, infecting him. From there the contagion had spread through bites. Flulike symptoms led to death, but then the dead came back. And all they wanted to do was eat other people.

"That's the exact date and time David was trying to reanimate Eduardo," Maggie said.

"I read a report where you documented what happened that night, how you believed something else had entered the Lazarus in addition to his soul," Jason said.

"Yes." Kimber couldn't help the shudder that went through her. "It knew me, and it was dark. Evil."

Maggie rested her elbows on her knees and studied Kimber. "I think it was the soul of Maddalene's vampire lover."

Kimber frowned. "How is that even possible?"

"Think about it. David—my necromancer master—didn't have enough power to finalize the raising. And when his power was cut off, the vampire soul went where the power was." She spread her hands. "You have always been the strongest, the best, of us. So it went to you and the Lazarus."

Was it possible? She'd never been able to come up with any explanation for how everything had gone so wrong that night. Could it be because of Maddalene's obsession with her dead lover? Raising murder victims to question them had become routine police work, so it wasn't unusual that more than one re-animation at a time would occur.

She was almost afraid to hope. "It wasn't my fault," she whispered. She lifted her gaze to the couple sitting across from her. "It really wasn't my fault."

Maggie and Jason both grinned and settled against the back of the sofa. "It really wasn't your fault," Maggie affirmed.

A sense of well-being flooded Kimber. God, she wasn't responsible for the zombie apocalypse. Wait until she told Duncan.

For the first time in months, things felt almost normal. She looked at Maggie. It was time to talk about something else. Time to focus on life instead of death. "When are you due?"

The other woman stroked a palm over her distended belly. "I'm finishing up my second trimester." She looked at Jason with a smile. "Thank goodness the first trimester is over. I had continuous morning sickness." She gave a wry grimace. "As in sick morning, noon, and night. It wasn't fun, especially when we had to move on to stay ahead of a horde."

"Well, you're safe here." Kimber glanced around the common area and saw that the three of them were the only ones left in the room. "I'll let you two go on to bed. Let the guards know if you need anything or if you want to see me. I'll try and stop by again soon."

After exchanging goodbyes, Kimber headed back to her suite. Duncan's office door was closed as she went by, so he must have been in that meeting with Vachon. She'd let him tell her how it went; then she'd spring her good news on him.

She took a quick shower and tumbled onto the bed, a wide

grin making her cheeks ache. God. She felt good, even if she hadn't gotten to smack anyone. She hadn't started the apocalypse, but she still wanted to stop it if she could. Now that there were two more necromancers here, she might finally have a real chance to try.

Chapter Three

"I agree," Duncan said to Xavier Vachon. They had been in conference for over an hour now and had hammered out a reasonable division of duties between their two enclaves. Now they talked about some of the details. "Zombies appear to be linear movers—they don't try to go up or under. Just straight ahead until something blocks their way. But if there are enough of them pushing against a fence, they could force it down. I want whatever we build to be sturdy enough to withstand a horde."

The other vampire steepled his fingers and settled more comfortably in the leather armchair in front of Duncan's desk. "I think going with concrete blocks would be our best bet. There's a manufacturing facility in Oakwood Village where we should be able to get supplies."

"Plus we can hit all the home improvement stores between here and Cleveland," Duncan said. "I doubt many people were carting off concrete blocks when they were looting at the onset of the Outbreak."

Xavier gave a small laugh. "Too true." Letting his hands rest on the arms of the chair, he crossed his legs. "We should construct a corridor roughly six feet wide, I think, with secured entrances every three hundred yards or so, on each side of the corridor so we can gain entry at specific points along the line."

"How tall were you planning on making the wall?"

"Oh, I thought six feet or so," Xavier said. "Tall enough they can't step over it, but not so tall that we can't see what's going on."

That was the height Duncan had had in mind. "If we need to get out, we can go up and over, right? I'm not sure openings are advisable."

"And if we're carrying injured? It's not impossible for our kind to heft someone over a six-foot wall, but at what cost to the injured person?"

Hmm. He had a point.

"Plus we may need to get out to scavenge, and hurling supplies over the wall may not be the optimal way to treat them." A slight smile curled his lips to take away the sting of his sarcasm.

"All right, all right. Your point is taken." Duncan grinned and gave a shake of his head. Xavier was intelligent and highly motivated to see to the safety of his people, just as Duncan was. And he recognized that both groups stood to gain much from this partnership. "My second, Atticus, is an excellent strategist. I'd like him involved in the actual design and construction of this corridor."

"I have no problem with that."

Duncan inclined his head in agreement.

"Now that that's out of the way," Xavier said, "I'd like to pick your brain about this donor system you have going on here."

"Ah. That caught your interest, did it?" He was proud that he'd come up with the idea, even if there were some kinks to be worked out.

Xavier raised one dark brow. "Not just mine. I met with Audra Shane recently. She expressed interest as well for the Toledo enclave." He leaned his head against the high back of the chair. "I imagine other vampire masters have heard of it, too."

Duncan gave a shrug. It wasn't a big deal. "It's something I've always wanted to do…well, if you consider 'always' being since the Outbreak." He grinned. "But if we have humans here willing to provide nourishment to us, we don't have to endanger ourselves with the hunt. And the humans are safer here than out there." He gestured toward the outer wall with its tall bank of windows.

"How do you convince them?"

"It helps that a few of the humans have been with us for the last eight or nine months and can attest that we're not vicious animals fanging everything in sight."

Xavier snorted. "That does seem to be the prevailing attitude, doesn't it?" He shook his head, his expression reflecting his dismayed amusement at the vagaries of humans. "Audra seemed to think it might be as simple as that. I'm not sure how much success she would have with it, though."

"Why do you say that? What's going on with her enclave?"

"They moved from Toledo to Put-in-Bay. Surrounded by water, they're quite safe from zombies, but the humans living there weren't too happy to suddenly be overrun by vampires." He stretched his legs in front of him. "We've set up a routine boat service between their island and our enclave, providing them with materials they need and food for the humans. That helps her cause. She sends me manpower as she can. Of course, being on an island means she's limited to the number of vampires and humans she can house, but she would still like information on your recruiting methods."

"I'll be happy to provide it, such as it is. All we do, really, is talk to them." He leaned back in his chair. "I have to be honest. Right now we're having problems with some of the humans. They resent being cooped up, even though it's for their own safety. They want to be allowed to go outside—to a park of all places. I'm not giving them permission, and that has some of them up in arms."

Xavier inclined his head. "I'll pass all that along. Now"—he set both feet on the floor and rested his elbows on his knees—"when do I get to meet the infamous Kimberly Treat?"

Duncan glanced at the brass carriage clock at the front of his desk. It was almost four o'clock, and he figured Kimber had gone to bed a while ago. She did her best to keep the same hours as he, but about two or so in the morning she started to peter out. "Why don't I show you to your room, and you can meet her once you've rested?" He paused. "You turned me down earlier, but can I fetch a bite for you?"

Xavier stood and stretched. "Have someone come to my room once I'm settled, would you?"

"Sure." Duncan came from around his desk and led the way

to the door. As he opened it, he saw Atticus walking toward him. "Just the person I wanted to see." When his second-in-command reached him, Duncan introduced him to their guest and said, "Would you get someone willing to feed Xavier?"

"Of course. If you'll excuse me," Atticus said with a slight bow and headed off.

"This way." Duncan motioned toward the opposite direction Atticus had gone. Walking past the door to his and Kimber's suite, he nodded to the guards and continued on his way. At a suite at the end of the hallway, he pushed open the door and gestured Xavier inside.

The other vampire entered the room and looked around. "Nice," he said.

"It used to be Maddalene's. We've done some redecorating," Duncan added, remembering the ostentation of the vampire queen's décor. Now it held dark wood furniture and seating in soothing blues and greens instead of the overabundance of reds and purples the queen had favored.

Xavier's lips twitched. "I imagine you did."

"That's right, you knew her."

"Hmm. Knew her and wasn't particularly a fan." He quirked a brow. "She had a hard-on for your necromancer, didn't she?"

Duncan didn't want to go into too many details; it was none of Xavier's business. But he didn't want to be rude and jeopardize their fledgling partnership. "She wanted Kimber's help with a reanimation. Kimber refused."

"Let me guess. She wanted to bring that bastard Eduardo back."

Duncan touched an index finger to his nose and then pointed to Xavier.

The other vampire wandered farther into the room. "That would have been disastrous. His head wasn't screwed on straight when he was human. Being turned into a vampire messed him up even more." He looked at Duncan. "Just out of curiosity, why did Kimber refuse?"

"She said it would take too much blood, too much power, to reanimate a corpse that had been dead over a hundred years. Also, whatever she brought back wouldn't really be Eduardo."

"And Maddalene wasn't having any of that."

Duncan shook his head. "No." Deciding that was enough, he said, "Let me know if you need anything. Atticus will bring you someone for nourishment." He opened the door. "Oh, and he will stay while you feed. Nothing personal."

Xavier gave a one-shouldered shrug. "Completely understood. You don't know me, so you can't be assured I won't go too far. I'd do the same in your place."

Duncan lifted his chin in acknowledgment and left the room. He was tempted to stop in and see Kimber, but at this hour he knew she was asleep. He headed back to his office. There were still a couple of hours before daybreak; he'd get some work done.

***

Kimber awoke with a gasp and shot upright in bed, her pulse thudding in her throat. The tendrils of the dream that had interrupted her sleep slid away, except for one lingering visual. Pregnant Maggie complaining about perpetual morning sickness.

She fought back rising nausea. Since when was just thinking about morning sickness enough to make her feel ill? She swallowed the bile rising in her throat, and swallowed again before she realized that she really was going to throw up. She bounded off the bed and rocketed into the bathroom, barely making it in time.

As she rose to her feet and reached for the mouthwash, she started counting days. Telling herself to not be silly, she realized how long it had been since she'd had a period and felt her skin go clammy. At least two months. She hadn't really thought about it until now, but even if she had, she would've assumed her lack of monthly bleeding was stress-related and not from the rare possibility of being pregnant with a vampire's child.

"God." She stared at her wan reflection in the mirrored medicine cabinet above the sink. "I can't be pregnant. Please don't let me be pregnant."

She had part of the Unseen in her. How would that affect a fetus?

First things first. She had to know for sure. Pregnancy tests weren't something vampires kept around, and she sure as hell had never thought she'd need one. But now she did, and that meant a trip to the nearest drugstore. The shelves were probably mostly empty, but how many looters had decided pregnancy tests were necessary items in an apocalypse?

She went back into the bedroom and threw on her clothes.

On her way through the living room, she picked up her trusty hatchet and slid the handle through a belt loop on her side. She opened the door and headed toward Duncan's office, glad that the two guards outside their suite didn't comment on the weapon hanging at her side.

Giving a perfunctory knock on the door, she pushed it open, glad to see Duncan was alone. "Hey."

His brows drew into a frown, and he got up and came around the desk. "Hey, yourself." He pulled her into a loose embrace and stared into her face. "What're you doing up?" Gently he pushed her back a little, his frown growing. "And why are you dressed like you're going out?"

"Because I am going out," she said with a smile. "I need—"

"Duncan," a deep voice intruded, "I hesitate to impose further upon your hospitality— Oh, I apologize. I didn't realize you had someone with you."

Kimber turned to see one of the most gorgeous men she'd ever laid eyes on hesitating just inside the room. He stood a few inches over six feet, with shiny black hair that fell to the top of his broad shoulders and dark blue eyes framed by thick lashes.

Duncan pulled Kimber to his side. "Xavier," he said with a smile. "You wanted to meet my very good friend Kimber Treat. Here she is."

Kimber shot him a glance. *Very good friend?* What the hell?

"Kimber, this is Xavier Vachon, leader of the Cleveland enclave."

She gave the model-gorgeous vampire a smile of welcome.

"It's a pleasure to meet you," she said, and shook the vampire's hand.

"The pleasure is mine," he responded with a slight smile curling his lips.

"I hope you and Duncan were able to make progress," she said.

"Yes, indeed." His gaze lingered on her face before dropping to her waist to light upon the hatchet. He met her eyes again. "You are braving the wilds, then?"

She nodded. "Yep. Need to run out for some…things."

Duncan placed one broad hand on her shoulder. "Kimber, we need to talk about this."

She glanced at him. "It's not a big deal. I just need…" She shot a look at Xavier. It was bad enough that she was going to flat-out lie to Duncan, but she was going to do it in front of another vampire king, and to top it off, the lie she was using was that she needed feminine hygiene products. There was no getting around it, so she just blurted it out. "I need tampons."

Duncan's nostrils flared as he drew in a breath. "You're not having your period."

Damn vampire sense of smell. "Not yet. I'm due to start any time." She held his gaze and tried to ignore the fact that they were talking about such a private thing in front of a stranger. "I can't sit around an enclave full of vampires and not have tampons, Duncan."

He looked at her, and finally a sigh left him. He glanced out the window. She followed his gaze to see the sky was lightening as dawn approached. "Fine," he said. "But take Atticus with you."

She leaned up and kissed him on the cheek. "Thanks. I will." Turning, she headed toward the door. "It was nice to meet you," she told Xavier as she passed him.

"You too," Xavier responded. As she pulled the door closed behind her, she heard him murmur, "If you have a moment, Duncan, I had another idea for the corridor."

Kimber ducked back into her rooms long enough to grab a backpack, then headed down to the security office on the ground floor. Atticus was there with two other vampires. "I need to hit a drugstore," she told him as she shrugged into the backpack. "Duncan wants you to go with me."

Atticus glanced at his wristwatch. "Give us a few minutes to get ready," he said.

"I'll wait in the lobby." Kimber walked out to the main receiving area and dropped onto a sofa. So far, so good. She really, really hoped the nearest drugstore, a couple of blocks away on Broadway, had what she needed. She didn't want to drag her posse of vampires all over town, especially if she found tampons at the first one. What excuse would she give to get them to go to another store?

She heard footsteps and looked up to see Atticus coming her way, the two guards behind him. "Let's go," he said.

She could tell from the look on his face that he'd double-checked her story with Duncan and wasn't happy being assigned babysitting duties. Oh well, sometimes it sucked being the second-in-command during a zombie apocalypse.

Sometimes it sucked being the possibly pregnant lover of a vampire during a zombie apocalypse, too.

Chapter Four

Her shopping trip proved to be successful. With several pregnancy test kits and a couple of bottles of prenatal vitamins—just in case—tucked into boxes of tampons she had in her backpack, Kimber and her companions were nearly back to the compound when she saw over a dozen zombies between them and the front gate. She sidled closer to Atticus. "Should we try heading around back?" she whispered, looking over his shoulder toward the path that led around the outside of the compound.

She caught one of the guards shaking his head before he said in a low voice, "There are more there. I can hear them."

Atticus's eyes narrowed. "Then here is where we fight our way through." He pulled the long sword from the scabbard secured between his shoulder blades. "Once the sound of battle reaches the guards along the fence, reinforcements will be sent out."

"You hope." Kimber pulled her hatchet free from her belt loop and got ready to whack some zombies. She'd really rather be whacking some moles, but this was the new reality.

The new reality was messy. And it sucked.

"I know they'll come and help." He shot her a glance. "Or more than just zombie heads will roll."

She appreciated his humor, especially since the first few shufflers caught sight of them and were headed their way. "Here we go," she said, and rushed forward. The three vampires, each holding swords nearly as long as she was tall, formed a line at her side.

The next several minutes passed in a blur of slashing, stabbing, and hacking. Kimber felt her aggression rising with each zombie she killed. The dark fragment of the Unseen within her eddied and flowed, lapping at her consciousness like an inexorable tide of malevolence. Sweat trickled between her breasts as much from her physical exertion as from the mental battle she waged to keep the evil energy from overpowering her.

She yanked her hatchet from the skull of the zombie she'd just put down. The force of her pull knocked her off balance, and she stumbled. She threw out her left arm to catch herself and felt Atticus's fingers curl around her hand.

Power surged through her, the Unseen that animated the vampire finding a connection with that inside Kimber. Her fingers clenched around his and her skin grew clammy with cold, then radiated heat. Unlike before, when she'd touched a zombie in order to draw upon the Unseen, there was no pain. Just a tremendous swell of energy. She hadn't meant to draw energy from Atticus, but now that she had, she was going to use it.

Gritting her teeth against the rising internal heat, yet strangely exultant from the darkness she sensed, she threw the malignant power out at the zombies. Little flashes of light danced across her field of vision as her blood pressure skyrocketed. So. Much. Power. It was alluring, the desire to hold on to that dark force. Why waste it on a bunch of zombies? She could use it herself.

But she needed more.

Aberrant pleasure rose within her, her spirit rejoicing in the nebulous energy coursing into her. Another flash of heat, and common sense returned. The last thing she wanted was to end up with even more of the Unseen in her. No, now that she'd started this, she had to finish it.

Her heart stuttered, then beat wildly in her rib cage. Through muffled hearing, she heard Atticus call her name, felt his attempt to dislodge her grip. She tried to unfurl her fingers but couldn't get them to cooperate. The zombies began to fall around them like marionettes with cut strings, lying as if boneless and certainly no longer animated in any way.

She let out a ragged sigh. Falling to her knees, she settled her rear on the backs of her calves. Only after the last zombie crashed to the ground was she finally able to release her hold on Atticus's hand. Now that her connection was lost, she was starting to feel the effect on her muscles as they started trembling. She turned her head toward him, realized he was on his knees, too. She groaned as the small movement made her head feel like it would explode. "Are you all right?" she asked in a raw voice.

"What the hell did you do to me?" His deep voice was raspier than normal and shaking with fatigue. She also didn't miss the fury there, either.

"I didn't mean to, Atticus," she tried to assure him. "It just happened."

His silvered gaze snared hers, and she couldn't look away. A muscle flexed in his jaw. "That doesn't make me feel any better about this," he said.

"I know. I'm sorry." Still shaken by light tremors, her arms and legs ached. She struggled to her feet without any help from the three vampires. She noticed they were all reluctant to touch her now. She didn't blame them. Even before the Outbreak, she'd wondered if her necromancy would enable her to control what animated vampires, since they were technically dead, just like the corpses she used to raise from the dead as part of her job. Now she knew, though she wasn't sure how much of this ability was due to her necromancy and how much of it was because of the Unseen within her.

Either way, she didn't like it at all.

"Listen, fellas, I don't like this any more than you do." She swayed and had to really focus to keep her feet beneath her. "But can we grouse about it back inside. Please?"

The two guards helped Atticus stand. He waved her on before him, and that was when she noticed they had indeed been joined by several other vampires to help fend off the zombies. They silently entered the gates of the compound.

As she walked across the lobby, she thought about the number of stairs she was going to have to climb and almost decided to stretch out on one of the sofas near the unused bank of elevators. But that would mean explaining to Duncan why she hadn't come upstairs and she had to think about that a bit.

So she kept putting one foot in front of the other and tried not to dwell on how tired she was or how much her body ached or how her head might just feel better if it weren't attached to her neck. Poor Atticus didn't look any better than she felt. When they reached their floor, she almost cried. Just a few more steps…well, okay, still a lot more, but in a few minutes she could collapse on the bed and die a little.

In front of her suite, she put out a hand to halt Atticus when he would have kept walking. He jerked away from her. She bit her lower lip and fought back the hurt. She couldn't blame him for his reaction. If she'd held on longer and had continued to sap his energy, she most likely would have killed him. "I'm sorry," she repeated. In a stronger voice, she said, "I promise I'll tell Duncan what happened. So please let me, all right?"

"What are you saying, Kimber? You're assuming I'm going to run and tattle on you?" His face, paler than normal, was as impassive as she'd ever seen it.

"Noooo," she drawled out slowly. She had assumed that, actually, but with the mood he was in she wasn't going to own up to it. "But I realize what a big deal this is. I'm just asking that you let him find out from me."

"Fine." He glanced at his watch. She noticed a slight tremble in his hand. He looked at her, his silver eyes hard and unforgiving. "This time of morning he's probably down with the new donor recruits. I'll at least let him know we've made it safely home." He glared at her before walking away without another word.

She sighed and, ignoring the questioning looks from the two

guards at her door, went inside her suite and headed straight to the master bathroom. She had blood on her and it had to come off. As much as she wanted to pee on a stick to see if she got one line or two, she had to get cleaned up first. And she needed to do all of it before Duncan came upstairs to go to bed.

Kimber took the fastest shower on record and then followed the instructions for the test. She set the stick next to the sink and walked into the bedroom. The little brochure indicated it could take up to two minutes for the results. How could such a short amount of time feel like so long?

She knew if she sat down, let alone got comfortable on the bed, she'd pass out, so she paced. And paced.

And paced. Stopped to look out the window at nothing and paced some more. Finally it was time. She walked back into the bathroom and looked at the stick.

Her heart jumped into her throat. Oh, God. Two blue lines. Maybe it was wrong. She sat on the toilet and dribbled enough to wet another test strip, with the same result. Half an hour later after a few glasses of water, a third result was the same.

Two. Blue. Lines.

She was pregnant. In the middle of a zombie apocalypse with a portion of the Unseen squatting in her body like an unwanted homesteader. What was she going to do?

The fatigue from taking on the Unseen finally became too much to fight, and she flopped onto the bed. Her thoughts nattered in circles until blessed oblivion fell over her.

* * *

Two days later, Kimber finally felt rested enough to actively think about the wreck of her life instead of merely worrying about it. She'd managed to give a plausible explanation to Duncan as to why she'd gone back to bed the day she'd gone out for feminine hygiene products. It helped that he was so focused on cleaning up the mess that Maddalene had left behind. He was dedicated to healing the enclave from her autocratic and cruel leadership and getting humans at least a little comfortable with the idea of being live donors for his vampires. He had so much on his mind right now that he'd accepted her explanation without question. That made her feel a little guilty, that she'd been able to deceive him so easily, not just once, but twice.

Now, just before sunrise, she sat in the living room of her and Duncan's suite. Pushing aside the fact she was pregnant for the moment, which was hard to do, she distracted herself by analyzing what she felt when she'd stripped power from Atticus.

All that malignant energy felt good. *She* felt good. Even as her body struggled to process that kind of power, almost buckling under the pressure, her mind, her spirit, had rejoiced in her ability to wield the darkness. That more than anything else scared her. Did she *want* to be evil? Was that what this was about? Was she being taken over by the dark side?

Even now, as she thought about who she was, who she wanted to be, she was excited by the idea of being able to hurt a vampire. Vampires were apex predators and Atticus was one of the most powerful she'd ever met, but if she had held on to Atticus longer, she could have really injured him, probably even fatally. There was a part of her, larger than she liked, that puffed up with pride at the thought. To take down a predator bigger and meaner meant *she* was the greatest.

She was sure it was the boost of power she'd gotten from him that had allowed her to push the Unseen out of the zombies. That extra power had given them true death. Granted, there had been only about fifteen or so, but still, it was something. It was a start. Her mind raced. If taking energy from Atticus allowed her to put down a couple handfuls of zombies, how many more could she have done with her hands on two vampires? And then two more? Just how many vampires could be sacrificed to stop the apocalypse? What would be too much?

Could there be too much?

What if Duncan were one of the ones she used?

Her breath hitched in her throat. No, no, no! She would never use Duncan that way. She'd have no reason to keep on going. She couldn't kill the father of her baby, even if it meant the threat of zombies was gone forever.

Could she?

She put one hand low on her abdomen where her little sprite nestled in safety and love. She'd only had a couple of days to get used to the idea, but she already loved the tiny fetus growing inside her and was determined to be the best mother she could. How would she be able to tell the little tyke that she'd killed its father?

There had to be another way.

She suddenly remembered the other two necromancers and realized there *was* another way. She wasn't sure how safe it would be for Maggie, as far along as she was in her pregnancy, and Kimber didn't want to do anything to jeopardize the safety of her own baby, but she also needed to get the Unseen out of her. If it was making her so crazy-aggressive, it couldn't be good for the baby. There was no other choice. Perhaps between her and Jason they could tap into the Unseen and pull it out of the zombies—and her—before sending it back where it belonged.

She'd go down and talk to Jason the first chance she got. She glanced at the grandfather clock standing in the corner near the fireplace. It was almost 9:00 a.m. She should go talk to them now. On some level she realized she couldn't keep avoiding Duncan—they did live together after all—but she could manage to be out of the suite when he came in to rest.

Kimber pushed to her feet and had taken only a few steps toward the door when it swung open. Duncan walked in and stopped when he saw her. Well, so much for avoiding him.

He moved forward and pulled her into his arms. He held her close, his face buried in her hair. "I've missed you the last couple of days," he finally said as he straightened to look down at her. "You're always gone when I come to bed." His lean hands came up to cup her face. Thumbs stroking across her cheeks, he said, "You look tired. And thinner. Are you all right? Should we find a doctor?" His brows drew down and he said, "With all the humans living here now, we should probably find a doctor anyway."

He looked so overwhelmed, which worried her. It was a look she'd never seen before and she didn't like it. "I'm fine," she said, nowhere near ready to tell him her news. It would only add more shadows to his face. Time for a distraction, for both of them. Regardless that she had things to tell him, they both needed this. Going up on tiptoe, she pressed a light kiss to his lips.

He took over, his hands tilting her head to give him the angle he wanted, and his tongue stroked over her bottom lip. When she opened her mouth, he surged inside, tasting her, teasing her. Carnal fire began to burn low in her gut, tightening her womb, making her sex wet and slick with arousal.

It was always like this with him. One touch, one kiss was all it took to rev her motor and make her burn for him.

Keeping his mouth on hers, Duncan swept her up into his arms and carried her to the bedroom. Once he'd set her on her feet, he made quick work of getting her clothes off, and even quicker work of his.

"I don't know how you manage to do that so fast," she said, and laughed.

"It's a talent," he bragged with a grin. He pushed her gently onto the bed and came down over her, his erection eager against her belly. He pressed slow kisses down the column of her throat, across one sloping collarbone before he took her nipple into his mouth and suckled. The motion shot straight to her clit, setting up an answering throb of desire.

The muscled width of his shoulders, speaking to the strength of this man, *her* man, called to her. She cupped her fingers around him, digging in her nails. He responded by sucking hard, drawing in as much flesh as he could. The rough silk of his tongue rasped over her swelling nipple, sending fiery shocks of exhilaration through her core. Her arousal flared and she cried out, tightening her grip on his shoulders. Duncan wrapped his arms around her and moved to her other breast with even more suction than before.

"Duncan!" Kimber struggled beneath him. It was too much; it wasn't enough. She didn't know if she could bear the excruciating torment he thrust upon her. But he wouldn't relent. As he continued to lave and suck, he moved one hand between her thighs. He moaned to find her sex so wet that the bed linens beneath her were damp.

He lifted his head and stared at her breasts. She looked down, too, to see both nipples were hard, so hard, and a deep, dark red from his ministrations. His fingers probed her folds, his thumb rubbing her clit, making her shudder and writhe against him.

"You're so responsive. I love you," he moaned, and slid a long finger inside her. He stroked in and out, added a second finger, then a third. He curled them, rubbing against the bundle of nerves in her sheathe.

As heady delight sizzled through her, she nearly shot off the bed. "Oh!" Desire and dark need furled within her. She scored her fingernails down his upper arms. "Oh, God, do that again."

He complied. She shoved her hips against his hand, rapture just out of her reach. Another thrust of his hand and she came, screaming his name. When she settled back down, he rubbed his cock through her slick folds and pressed the tip of his shaft inside her sheath. As he thrust forward, working his way into her swollen sex, he slid his forearms under her knees, lifting her butt off the bed, giving him all the control. With each downward stroke, his pelvis struck her puffy clit, sending intense slivers of pleasure through her groin.

Duncan kept moving, pulling out and slamming back in with increasing speed and force. The slap of his balls against the rounded curve of her buttocks, the feel of his hard cock shoving in and out of her, the way his lean body moved above her all made her want more.

"Harder!" she cried, trying to shove against him. But with her legs draped over his arms, leaving only her upper back and head on the mattress, she had no way to direct how this went.

Thankfully he moved faster, putting more power behind each thrust. His big body slammed against her, each lunge driving desperate moans from her. Another orgasm loomed, tantalizing her with its nearness. Need seethed. She tried to buck into his thrust and whimpered when the position he had her in made it impossible. If he didn't give her what she wanted, and soon, she was going to hurt him. She was appalled to feel that way, but the desire twisted with the darkness inside her, making it difficult to tell which was which. "Please, Duncan," she begged.

"All right, love." He let one of her legs drop to the bed and brought his hand to her sex. His face hard with his own need, hips driving into her like a piston, he pinched her clit, then rubbed it in circles.

It was enough. Lightning shot through every cell. Every muscle tensed, her body heaved. Her insides twisted like a dishrag being rung dry. Then with a scream Kimber flew apart, spasms seizing her with such strength she bowed and shook. When she fell back to reality, it was to find Duncan in the midst of his own climax, jerking and groaning. His cock pulsed inside, filling her with his release. With the speed of a striking snake, he bent over her and sank his fangs into the side of her throat.

She cried out and strained up in another orgasm, her sex milking her lover of every last drop. After a final pump of his hips, he held still, then finally lifted his head and released her other leg. He collapsed onto her, his arms closing around her to hold her close. With a low groan, he rolled onto his back, keeping her imprisoned in his arms, his softening cock still snuggled in her sheath.

She gasped against him and fought to learn how to breathe again. Streaks of red caught her eye and she lifted up to look at his arms. Bloody furrows raked the entire length of his upper arms, from shoulder to elbow, four rows on each arm. She sat up and looked down at her hands. Blood and skin was crammed beneath her nails. "Oh my God."

Her stomach roiled and bile rose in her throat. She really *had* hurt him. With a low grunt, she rolled off the bed and retrieved the first-aid kit from the medicine cabinet in the bathroom. Coming back to the bed, she motioned for him to sit up. "Let me take care of those."

He shrugged but shifted to put his back against the headboard. "I'll heal. You don't need to do that." He gestured to the gauze and bottle of hydrogen peroxide in her hands.

"I'll feel better." She'd done this to him, used her nails to groove out his flesh. At the time she'd been aware of her movement, just not the end result. As she began to clean his wounds, she had the urge to press down harder, to cause even more pain. What the hell was wrong with her?

* * *

Duncan watched Kimber tend to the wounds she inflicted and wondered at her attitude. This was the second time they'd made love in the last few days, and both times he'd seen her struggle to contain a new level of aggression. She wouldn't talk to him about it, though, and it was making him crazy. How could he be an effective leader if he couldn't even help his own lover?

He waited until she'd capped the bottle of peroxide and set the first-aid kit on the bedside table before he said, "Talk to me, Kimber. Tell me what's going on with you."

She heaved a sigh and got to her feet. Going over to his dresser, she pulled out one of his T-shirts and slipped it over her head. She usually wasn't uncomfortable being nude around him, so her action told him what they were about to deal with wasn't going to be pleasant. Was she tired of being with him? Had he been too dominant in their lovemaking?

"Kimber?" The waiting was hell on his nerves.

"The day before yesterday, when we went out for tampons?" She glanced at him. When he nodded, she went on. "You know on our way back we were attacked by zombies."

"Yes, Atticus told me. I came up here to see how you were doing, but you were already asleep. I didn't want to wake you. Then you were gone later that night when I woke up." He watched her to gauge her reaction.

She gave a slight wince. "Yes, well, I had things to do." She waved one hand in the air. "That doesn't matter. What does matter is that when we were fighting the zombies, I stumbled, and when I flung out my arm to try to keep my balance, I ended up grabbing hold of Atticus." She looked at him. "Atticus didn't tell you any of this?"

He frowned. "He told me you had to fight zombies, that you were successful, and everyone was all right. Was there more he should have told me?"

She shook her head. "No. I mean, there was more, but I asked him to let me tell you." She blew out a breath. "When I grabbed him, I drew energy from him and it allowed me to push the Unseen out of the zombies. You should have seen them drop to the ground."

"You did what?" He straightened from his slouched position against the headboard. He couldn't have heard her right. She attacked his second-in-command?

"I didn't do it on purpose," she said. "He must have seen me stumble and reached out to help me at the same time I flung my hand out. Once I had hold of him and the power transfer started, I couldn't let go. I tried, Duncan." Her eyes went round and pleading, and her lower lip got a slight tremble to it. "It hurt, just like before, but it…" She clamped her jaw shut.

"It what?"

"It felt good, too. It was power, and it was mine." She began to pace the room, her hands gesturing wildly. "This could be something big, Duncan. If all necromancers have this ability, we could end the apocalypse."

He got off the bed and pulled on his jeans. "And just how many vampires do you propose we sacrifice?"

She came to a stop and stared at him. "It wouldn't have to be a sacrifice. I didn't kill Atticus."

"But you came close, didn't you? Or you could have," he amended. At her stubborn expression, he said, "I know you, Kimber. I know the kind of power you have. Plus you have some of the Unseen in you. How did that affect what happened with Atticus? Or did it happen with Atticus *because* of the Unseen in you?"

Her shoulders slumped. "I don't know."

He studied her for a minute, then left the bedroom. He strode through the living room and yanked open the door to the hallway. "Find Atticus and bring him here," he said to the guards. Without waiting for a response, he closed the door. When he turned around, he saw Kimber standing in front of the sofa, twisting her fingers together. She'd pulled on her jeans but still wore his T-shirt.

Her auburn hair, tousled and silky-looking, cascaded around her shoulders. "I didn't do it on purpose, Duncan," she whispered. Her teeth dug into her lower lip. "I wouldn't do something like that. You have to believe me."

"I'd like to believe you, sweetheart. I would." He walked over and put his hands on her shoulders, giving them a slight squeeze. "But I've seen how you've changed. I've seen you fight whatever is rising in you. I think if a situation presented itself and you believed taking energy from a vampire was the only solution, I'm not sure you could stop yourself."

A knock sounded on the door, and it swung open to reveal Atticus.

"Come in," Duncan invited. When the door closed behind his second-in-command, Duncan said, "Kimber just told me what happened on your way back from the drugstore."

Atticus shot a glance her way but said nothing.

"This is a serious development," Duncan went on, "and poses a potential threat to all vampires. I want all necromancers under guard until further notice. Let everyone know they're considered dangerous and should not be touched under any circumstances."

Atticus inclined his head. "Understood and agreed." With another glance at Kimber, he departed.

"Does that include me?" Kimber asked, her voice hard. "Am I to be kept under guard? Am I not to be touched?"

He clenched his teeth. "If you're not with me, then, yes, you will have a guard. And anyone else will be advised not to touch you, but you and I will definitely be skin to skin, sweetheart. You can count on that."

"Don't be so sure," she said. "I'm not just any other necromancer, Duncan. I'm the woman who loves you. The woman you claim to love." Her fists clenched at her sides and he had the distinct impression she was fighting throwing a punch at him. After a few seconds she let out a little growl and headed back toward the bedroom. Over her shoulder she threw out, "You're treating me like a monster. The way I'm feeling right now, that might be an accurate assessment. You might not be safe from me."

Chapter Five

The next week rolled by and tensions between the vampires and the necromancers grew. Kimber's guilt over keeping the baby a secret from Duncan wore on her nerves, and her frustration over her inability to fix the situation increased. Over iced tea early one evening, she talked to Natalie about the latter.

"I just don't know what you can do," her friend told her. "I mean, ultimately Duncan's the one in charge. Until he believes none of you are a threat to his people, the damned guards stay." She gestured toward the tall, bulky vampire standing to one side of the door. "No offense, Leon," she said.

"None taken," came the calm reply.

Kimber folded her arms across her chest and glowered at the vampire before turning her gaze to Natalie. "Despite what Duncan says," Kimber whispered, "he hasn't touched me in a week. I think I'm in withdrawal."

"Sex withdrawal?" At Kimber's nod, Natalie barked a laugh.

"Welcome to the majority of the world, hon. At least, welcome to my world."

Before Kimber could respond to that or give Leon a hard time over his discomfort in listening to them talk about their sex lives, or lack thereof, someone knocked on the door. He opened it to the guards on the other side. "Duncan has asked that Kimber and Natalie join him in his office."

Kimber stood. "Did he say why?"

"No."

Motherfu…This was getting ridiculous. He wouldn't touch her and now he was sending for her like she was one of his minions? This was so not going to be the way things went from now on. "Come on, Nat," she ground out. "His Highness has summoned us."

"Oh, boy." Natalie got up from the sofa and followed Kimber to Duncan's office.

When they walked in, Kimber saw a tall, willowy blonde standing by the bank of windows. Her posture and clothing reminded her of Aodhán. She looked toward the big mahogany desk. Duncan was seated behind it and Atticus stood to his side. And there just in front of Atticus was her fey friend. "Aodhán!" She gave a screech of welcome and threw herself at him.

His arms came around her in a tight hug. It was the first time in seven days she'd felt someone's arms around her, and it brought the pain of the growing distance between her and Duncan that much closer to the surface.

"*Mo chara.*" Aodhán rested his cheek against the top of her head. "I am so happy you're all right."

"Yeah, I'm fine, too," Natalie called out. "Just in case you were worried. Which you probably weren't, since you've been gone so long."

Kimber pulled away from Aodhán. "Go easy on her," she whispered. She had no doubt Duncan could hear her, and maybe even the fey woman by the windows, but Natalie wouldn't be able to. "She's really missed you."

"As I have her." He looked at Natalie. In a louder tone, he said, "I am glad to know you're fine, Natalie. I had no doubt that my friend Duncan would keep you safe."

"Hmph." She crossed her arms. "What's all this about?"

Duncan motioned to the leather armchairs in front of his desk. "Please, sit."

After Kimber and Natalie sat down, Aodhán said, "I come with dire news. The imbalance in the Unseen has spread to the fey realm. It's in its early stages, but all signs indicate it will be as big as what you have here. Brigid"—he gestured toward the fey woman—"is able to focus supernatural power. Think of her as a collector that gathers your powers and then sends them back out in one concentrated beam. She is most successful when dealing with triangular sources. We believe she could do the same for you." He looked at Kimber. "We need your help."

There was silence while Kimber digested the news. Then Natalie said, "Oh, this is rich. When we asked you for help, you told us to go screw ourselves, that the problems of the human realm were no concern of the fey. Now you have the balls to ask us for help?"

"Natalie." Duncan's voice held a warning note. Even Atticus had stiffened.

Aodhán waved them off. "No, no, it's all right. I understand how she feels. If the situation were reversed, I'd most likely feel the same way."

Kimber shot to her feet. "We really need to take care of this, Duncan. Now. I'm not sure how, but I think I need to start with Maggie and Jason. And Brigid, of course, if she can do what's claimed."

Duncan narrowed his eyes. "I'm not sure that's a good idea."

"What's the matter, you afraid we're going to take over the world?" She scowled. "The only ones who'll be able to push the Unseen out of the zombies and back into itself are necromancers. Manipulating the Unseen is what we do. Maybe Brigid can keep us focused so we don't accidentally yank any Unseen out of your people while we're fixing humanity's problem."

He didn't like her attitude, she could tell. Tough. He shouldn't have been treating her like a leper for the last seven days.

"Fine. But you'll still have guards."

"Oh, I wouldn't expect anything less. And I'll make sure to remind them they're not to touch us. Save you the trouble." With a deeper glower, she turned on her heel. "Come on, Leon," she said to her guard. She looked at the fey woman. "You coming?"

When the woman walked toward her, Kimber nodded and headed to the door, her vampire guard on her heels.

* * *

Natalie watched them go. Feeling suddenly shy and unsure, she got to her feet. "Um, I guess I'll go, too."

"Wait, please." Aodhán walked over to her and looked down into her face. "We need to talk."

Yes, they did. She just wasn't sure she wanted to hear what he had to say. He'd walked away and only returned because their little zombie problem had bled over into the fey realm. She rubbed at the pain in her chest. He hadn't come back for her.

That wasn't the behavior of a man in love, not in any book she'd ever read.

She glanced at Atticus. He hadn't fed in several days and she knew he had to be hungry. He shook his head and jerked it toward the door, giving her permission to leave. "Come to my room," she murmured to Aodhán, and led the way.

When the door to her room one floor down closed behind them, she motioned him toward the plush teal-colored sofa in the living room. The floor plan to her room was like a loft. It was large and open, with the living room flowing into her bedroom area, the two rooms separated only by a half wall. The other side of the living room led into the kitchen, with a small dining room off to the side. The bathroom was the only self-contained room, and it was just large enough for a toilet, sink, and tub with a shower. It had suited her needs, but with Aodhán taking up so much space, it seemed too small now.

She sat down on one end of the sofa and watched him lower

himself to the opposite end. God, he was gorgeous. His dark hair was pulled back into a ponytail with those ever-present small braided sections at his temples, also caught in the tie holding his hair back. He wore leather pants and a supple ice-blue shirt that buttoned partway down. The neck was open, allowing some of his dark chest hair to show. His sword in its scabbard hung from his left hip. His bright blue eyes focused on her, making her fight the urge to squirm.

"You said you wanted to talk," she prodded him. God, she'd missed him so much, but she'd thrown herself into her new responsibilities here at the enclave, making herself so tired she hadn't had much time to think. Besides, he'd been the one to walk away, not her. As a matter of fact, she'd chased him down and pretty much begged him to stay only to be shot down. She was under no obligation to make this easy on him, especially if he was going to break her heart again.

He leaned toward her and cupped her face. His thumb ran across the fading bruise on her cheek. "What happened here?"

His light touch sent shivers through her, weakened her resolve to remain stoic. Unmoved. She drew away, and he dropped his hand and leaned back into the sofa. "I had a difference of opinion with someone," she murmured. "His face looks worse than mine."

Aodhán stayed silent for a moment. "I don't like the sound of this. Who was it?"

"It's okay. I'm fine. Nothing you need to concern yourself with." An awkward silence spread between them.

"I never meant to hurt you, Natalie," he finally said, his voice soft and husky. It rasped across her senses and made goose bumps pop up along her arms.

Damn him. What kind of fey magic did he have to make her respond so easily? She scowled at him.

"I hadn't planned on being gone as long as I was." He brought one leg up and twisted to face her, leaning forward to brace one forearm across his thigh. "Time moves differently in the fey realm than it does here. For me, only a little over a week has passed."

"But you knew more time was passing out here, didn't you? You knew it had been a month and a half? I know it doesn't seem like a long time, but when there was no word from you, I thought—"

He sighed. "Yes, I knew. And I worried about you."

She wanted to believe him, she did. She just didn't want to get hurt.

He went on. "But I couldn't get away before now. It has taken me several days to convince our rulers that we'd need humans' help to battle back the Unseen and the effects it has had on our realm."

"Just what effects are you talking about?"

"We don't have zombies, thank the Makers, but we are losing magic. It's as if the Unseen is sucking it up like a sponge. Our best philosophers have determined it is using our magic to continue to fuel the apocalypse here. If we can stop the zombies in the human realm, our realm will also be saved. That's our greatest hope, anyway." He reached out and took her hands in his. "I would have come back sooner if my people hadn't been in such danger, Natalie. You must believe me."

At his words, much of her anger retreated. She swallowed.

"Why?" she asked in a whisper. "Why would you have come back? To help protect Kimber?" As far as she knew, that was the only reason he'd stayed to begin with. Other than tease her with sexual innuendos, especially about his mighty sword, he'd never really showed a lot of interest in her until right before he'd left. And then he'd left anyway. Oh, she realized it was necessary. He had to help his people. It just wasn't fair.

"For you, *grá mo chroí*. I would have come back for you. Kimber is merely my friend."

She stared down at their joined hands, then looked into his face. Sincerity blazed from his eyes. Her pulse skittered. "What does that mean, *grá mo chroí*?"

"Love of my heart." He let go of her hands and cupped her face. "You are my heart, Natalie. The reason it beats, the reason I draw breath."

"You have a funny way of showing it." She drew away from him and stood, putting distance between them. She couldn't think when he touched her. "You kissed me like you thought you'd never see me again. You can't sit there and tell me you planned on coming back when you left the last time and expect me to believe it. If it weren't for the problem with the Unseen in your realm, you wouldn't be here now. At least admit that much."

Or was she just being a selfish, frustrated bitch?

He stood, too, but didn't come any nearer. "I won't lie to you. At the time I was leaving, I thought I would never leave the fey realm again. I thought I would go home and be able to forget about you. Get on with my life. Find a nice fey girl to fall in love with."

She narrowed her eyes. This she didn't want to hear. At all. "You're such a jackass."

He ignored that. "But as time went by, I realized I wasn't forgetting you. You had worked your way under my skin, into my heart, and you weren't budging. I had no life if you weren't in it. There weren't any fey girls to fall in love with, because I had no more love to give. It's all yours."

Her heart thumped a staccato beat against her ribs and thrummed wildly in her throat. Dare she believe him? "Those are some awfully pretty words, Aodhán." From an awfully pretty man. She shook her head. "I'm afraid to believe you," she finally whispered what was in her heart.

"I know, *mo chroí*. I'm sorry for that, and I mean to prove you can believe what I say. That you can believe *in me*." He came closer then and drew her into his arms. "There is a human saying that actions speak louder than words. If you have trouble with what I say, then believe this."

He slanted his mouth over hers, lips coaxing her to open. When she parted on a gasp, his tongue surged in. One big hand wrapped around her nape, holding her head where he wanted it, and the other grasped her hip to pull her lower body closer. The hard ridge of his erection pressed against her belly with only a few layers of clothing separating them. It was just like that last kiss all over again.

With a low moan, Natalie twisted away from him. She blinked back tears. "No! You can't just waltz in here and kiss me, then expect me to fall into your arms. You hurt me," she yelled. "You kissed me, like you just did, and then you left."

He held himself stiffly. "I had an obligation to my people," he said.

"I understand that." She wrapped her arms around her waist. "So what's to keep those obligations from making you leave me again?"

His expression softened. "I've explained my...situation to the rulers, and they have accepted it. If I leave the human realm to return to the fey, you will go with me."

She blinked. And frowned. "I can't just up and go to the fey realm."

"Why not?" He glanced around her apartment. "This is nice, but you live among vampires, surrounded by zombies. Once the zombie threat is eliminated, why would you continue to live here? We could still come back to visit your friends, if that's what's worrying you." His dark brows drew down. "Unless it's Atticus? That's it, isn't it? I saw the way you exchanged looks with him. What does he mean to you?"

She almost told a fib, that she and Atticus were lovers, just to see how he'd react, but it would be done only out of pure cussed meanness, and she wasn't going to sink that low. "We're friends, like you and Kimber."

"I think he'd like to be more than that."

She shrugged. "Maybe." She knew she had to tell him the rest. Even if she and Atticus had never had sex, sharing her blood with him lent an intimacy to their relationship she knew Aodhán didn't have with Kimber. "I'm his personal donor."

Aodhán's eyes darkened. "You give him your blood?"

Natalie nodded. "There's nothing sexual about it," she hastened to add.

"He lets you feel the pain of the bite, then?" He moved closer. His hands in fists at his sides, he asked, "Or does he allow his vampire glamour to turn the pain into sensual pleasure?"

She heaved a sigh. "Okay, okay. He does that, but I don't..." Her cheeks flared with heat and she had a feeling she was as red as a boiled lobster. "I've never, you know, come from it." She scowled. "And, anyway, you weren't here, weren't even planning on coming back, so it's really none of your business anyway."

This was not the sort of conversation she'd ever expected to have with Aodhán. Damn it. How embarrassing.

He leaned back on his heels. "Well, at least he doesn't give you an orgasm while he feeds." His scowl matched hers. "I don't like the thought of him touching you in any way." He reached out and slowly drew her back into his arms. "Just give me another chance, *mo chrot.* That's all I ask."

She rested her cheek against the hard muscles of his chest. She was so afraid he'd walk away from her again, and she wasn't sure how she'd get through it a third time. He'd asked her to give him another chance. How could she?

How could she not? If he left, she'd be heartbroken, but at least she would have tried. One thing the apocalypse had shown her about herself was that she wasn't a coward. She refused to start acting like a scaredy-cat now.

So she'd give him another chance. And if he hurt her, maybe she'd just bust his balls before she let him walk away from her again.

Chapter Six

I think we can all agree that the situation is worse than we ever dreamed it could be," Jason said. He sat beside Maggie, the fingers of one hand twined with hers, his other hand covering hers comfortingly.

Kimber stared at him, then looked down at her own hands, fingers twisting in her lap. She was acutely aware of Leon standing several paces behind them, close enough to hear their conversation even if they whispered but not close enough to be touched. The fey woman Brigid perched on the edge of a folding chair situated between the sofa and the armchair upon which Kimber was seated. As of yet, she hadn't contributed to the conversation. If anything, she'd seemed completely disinterested in the discussion up to this point.

Kimber focused on the ongoing conversation. "Yes, if the fey realm has been affected, and I have no reason to doubt what Aodhán has told me, then we're SOL."

"It is as he said," Brigid murmured, her voice holding a note of censure, probably for Kimber's apparent lack of faith in Aodhán. "Day by day our magic wanes, siphoned off by the Unseen." Her gaze flitted over the necromancers before it settled once more upon Kimber. "Without our magic, we will die. It is what sustains our realm. It is everything to us."

"So what do we do?" Maggie leaned forward, never letting go of Jason's hands.

Kimber paused. It would be so much easier to practice using a vampire, but she knew that would never happen. Plus she didn't want to put any of Duncan's people at risk. This was still such an unknown. She explained to Maggie and Jason about her previous experience in drawing upon the Unseen to fell zombies. "But it's not easy, and it's very draining. The first time I tried to draw the Unseen out of a friend who'd been bitten, I almost died."

Maggie and Jason took a few moments to mull that over. Then Maggie said, "Tell us what to do, and when do we start?"

Kimber drew in a deep breath. This was where things got a bit murky. "I'm honestly not even certain this will work. I've never tried to join my power with other necromancers. But I think it can be done. Except…" She looked at Maggie. "I'm not so sure *you* should do anything." She motioned vaguely toward the pregnant woman's midsection. "I don't want you to do something that could jeopardize your baby."

The other woman frowned and, disengaging one of her hands from Jason's grip, placed a palm protectively over her belly. "Nor do I, but how does practicing my craft—doing my job—put my baby in jeopardy?"

"With what I think we'll need to do, it very well could. It will take a tremendous amount of energy, even energy that would ordinarily be given to your baby as a natural process of childbearing." Kimber briefly closed her eyes. Now was the time she should tell them that she carried around some of the Unseen within her and let them know how it was affecting her mood. She didn't want to verbalize it, though, because now that she was pregnant, too, it made it all the more real. Logic told her that whatever might put Maggie's baby in danger would surely have the same effect on her baby.

"Just what is it you think we need to do?" This from Jason, who looked as concerned as Maggie did.

There was no hope for it. Kimber had to come clean. At least partially. She cleared her throat. "Just to be sure we're all on the same page, you are aware that the Unseen is what's animating the zombies, right?"

They both looked startled. Brigid looked bored once again with the chitchat going on around her. Damned fairies. Nothing was important until it affected them directly.

"You didn't know?" Kimber frowned.

Maggie and Jason exchanged a look and shook their heads. "No," Maggie said. "I thought it was a virus, since it's spread by bite." Her expression became uncertain. "You know, like in the movies."

"Right," Jason contributed. "That's what I thought, too. You're saying it's not that way?"

Kimber suddenly felt like she'd been all alone in this battle, even though there were other necromancers all over the world.

Maybe she was more aware because she'd seen the initial attack? "It is spread by bite, yes. Patient Zero, Lazarus, was the one who bit the ME, who then spread the zombie phenomenon, for want of a better word. But the origins are from the Unseen, not a virus."

"And you've been able to push it out of them?" Maggie glanced at Jason again and Kimber saw her fingers tighten around his hand.

"Yes."

Maggie's eyes widened. "Were you touching a zombie when you did it? How did it feel? Did it hurt?"

"It hurt." Kimber leaned forward. "Doing this puts a great strain on your system. I can't stress that enough. It's different than tapping into the Unseen to animate a corpse for questioning. That's a piece of cake because you still have a spark of the person's soul to work with, to anchor the Unseen to. But now, with everything so messed up…" She shook her head and sighed. "It's not like it used to be."

She almost volunteered the information about what she'd done to Atticus but thought better of it. She didn't know how these two felt about vampires, and she didn't want to give them any ideas. The last thing she needed was for them to go around attacking vampires.

The other woman looked hopeful when she asked, "Does it reverse the process? It makes them human again?"

"No." Seeing the disappointment on Maggie's face made Kimber feel like she'd just kicked a cute, fuzzy kitten. Nevertheless, she wouldn't do either of them any favors if she wasn't direct. "The initial infection kills them, Maggie. When the Unseen is stripped out of them, they go back to their original state, which is being dead."

"Oh." The word came out in barely a whisper.

"I'm sorry." Kimber didn't know what else to say. Everyone had someone who'd been turned...well, except for Kimber. She had no family and the one friend she'd had who'd been attacked had been killed before he could turn into one of those mindless cannibals.

"How did you do it?" Jason asked, twining his fingers with Maggie's.

"The procedure is much the same as you would use for a raising. Only instead of summoning the Unseen to inhabit a body, you summon it to leave a body. Or bodies, more accurately." Kimber studied them carefully. Both seemed to be following her reasoning, even if they looked a little shell-shocked. "I've only been able to do it once without holding on to a zombie, and it..." She swallowed. "Well, let's just say it's easier doing it by starting with one zombie."

"You're saying we have to do this one at a time?" Maggie's frown crinkled her forehead.

"Not exactly. You start with one but spread it, like an infection." She gave a small smile. "We fight infection with infection."

Brigid sat up straighter. "Yes, I understand your thought process on this." She gave an abrupt nod. "I would be able to assist in this endeavor." Her gaze flicked over the other two necromancers. "My power acts as a focus. Think of me as a prism, anchoring three separate laser beams into one more powerful beam."

It felt weird for one of the fey to be talking about laser beams, but that was the kind of world Kimber lived in now. Ten minutes later, impatient with going over the same talking points again and again, Kimber came to a decision. "We need to practice."

Jason stood and rested clenched fists on his hips. "You want us to go out into a bunch of zombies? And do…what? Hold their hands and sing 'Kumbaya'? Are you nuts?"

"No, no." This was getting them nowhere. Kimber stood, too, and added, "Look, let me talk to Duncan. There has to be a safe way we can do this."

"*Safe* and *zombies* really shouldn't be together in the same sentence," Maggie muttered.

Kimber couldn't stop a quick grin. "We'll find a way. I'll get back to you." As Brigid got to her feet, Kimber turned toward the door and saw Leon. Her smile faltered. She'd actually forgotten about him for a few minutes. "Come on, Leon," she said on an aggrieved sigh. "Take me to your leader."

He shot her a disgruntled look that almost made her want to apologize. Almost. She recognized that he was just doing his job and that she was really upset with Duncan, not Leon. But she felt like she'd choke on any apology she might try to give, so she kept her mouth shut.

When they reached the lobby, she saw she'd been in the human section long enough for the sun to set and full dark to fall. They crossed to the stairs that led up to the other floors,

Kimber leading the way with Leon and Brigid following silently behind. As they approached Duncan's office, she looked at Leon and said, "Why don't you show Brigid to her quarters? I'm sure she'd like to rest a bit, maybe freshen up." She glanced at the fey woman. "Would you like something to eat? I'm sorry I didn't think to ask you that before."

Why could she apologize to this stranger without blinking but not the vampire who'd been part of her personal protection detail for the last month? God, something was royally screwed up with her.

"I'm not hungry, but I would like to rest, thank you."

Leon hesitated outside the door to Duncan's office.

"Oh, come on, Leon. I sleep in the same bed with Duncan without any guards standing by. He'll be fine with you letting me go into his office by myself."

The big vampire folded his arms over his chest and broadened his stance. "So, go inside his office, and then I'll escort Brigid to her room."

Kimber pursed her lips. "Don't trust me either, eh?" Jerk. None of them seemed to want to believe her when she said what happened with Atticus had been an accident. She was glad now that she hadn't apologized. "Fine." She threw up her hands and gave a brief knock. At Duncan's bid to enter, she opened the door and waggled her fingers at Leon. "Off you go now." Without waiting to see his response, she pulled the door closed behind her and walked toward where Duncan sat behind his desk.

He looked up. There was a hint of reserve in his eyes, something she'd never thought she'd see with him. For all his talk about knowing she'd never hurt him, he sure wasn't putting his money where his mouth was. "How'd things go with the other necromancers?" he asked. His deep voice never failed to ignite her engines, but the same glimmer of constraint in the low tones dashed ice over the fire.

Really, could she blame him for his hesitancy? With the way her mood swung toward aggression, who was to say she might not go off and try to siphon off his energy? She'd never wanted this strong man, this alpha vampire, to feel fear around her, and that he might broke her heart.

With that in mind, her response was muted. "Fine. We want to practice on some zombies. I thought maybe we could—"

"No way in hell!" He shoved his chair back and stood. One palm slammed down on the desktop. His features hardened with resolve. "It was one thing to let you go out to get tampons, which you needed. I'm not about to risk my people so you and your little friends can go play with zombies. Hell, what is it with you humans wanting to go waltzing around like there's no danger out there? Or, worse, expecting me to put my people in jeopardy to protect you while you play?"

She realized right away that he was being an ass because he was still shaken over what she'd done to Atticus, though that didn't make her feel any better about his attitude. She also realized he must have received more complaints from the humans in "the hole," as they'd taken to calling the basement level. But fury over his condescending attitude blasted away any sympathy she felt or any guilt she held in lying to him about those damned tampons. "We're not in second grade," she gritted out. "I'm not talking about going outside and playing a game of tag. Or taking a walk in the park," she added to let him know what this was really about.

She really wanted to yell at him, maybe even bop him a good one right on his schnoz, but that wouldn't make him more agreeable. She put her hands on her hips and fought to keep from tapping her foot in agitation. "I'm talking about setting up a practice area, something that won't put the compound at risk. We could set up an arena of sorts in one of the buildings that's unused on this block. Build a fenced-in corridor to get us from here to there safely, and we could handle the rest."

"And just how would you get your zombies to this arena?" Duncan sat back down with a frown. At least he seemed to be listening to her instead of reacting to her words. "If it still comes down to vampires going out to round them up—"

"No, it doesn't. Jason and I could—"

"Absolutely not. There's no way in hell I'm letting you endanger yourself, either. And who the hell is Jason?" He jumped to his feet again, his frown deepening into a scowl, silver sparking the green of his irises.

Rather than anger her, the evidence of his jealousy knocked down a few chunks in the wall she'd begun to build around her emotions where he was concerned. Maybe there was a road back to when they'd been happy with each other. She gave a soft smile and walked around his desk to plop herself down in his lap. Her smile widening at his startled look, she wrapped her arms around his neck and whispered, "Jason's one of the necromancers and he's madly in love with Maggie, the other one." She stared down into his eyes. "If we do this, and I think we should, I'm afraid it's me or your vamps, lover. Your choice."

He stared at her for a moment; then his shoulders slumped. "Well, if I agree to let you do this, I guess it'll be a couple of my vamps." He brought one hand up and cupped her face, rubbing his thumb gently across her cheek. "I don't want to lose you, Kimber." For the first time in a week she could see in his eyes, his face, exactly what he felt—desire, uncertainty, and so much love it took her breath away.

And just like that, any lingering frustration and anger melted away. She leaned forward and pressed her lips to his. It was soft and sweet and gentle, a slow sliding of her mouth against his. He closed his lips around her lower one, then the upper before settling firmly over her mouth again. She sighed, parting her lips. He slipped his tongue inside her mouth, tasting her, caressing her tongue in slow, easy strokes. She loved his flavor, though she always had a hard time describing it. Salty, with a little hint of sweet. Primitive with a definite undercurrent of ultramasculinity.

She moaned. Duncan responded with a moan of his own and held her tighter, his tongue twining around hers with greater force. She arched against him, rubbing her tingling breasts against his hard chest. At some point she needed to breathe, and she broke away from him. *This* was what she'd missed this last week, this closeness, the carnality behind their love.

"I love you," she told him.

"I love you, too," he replied with a light kiss to her mouth. He settled her more comfortably on his lap and wrapped his arms around her to clasp his hands over her hip. After a few moments of companionable silence, he asked, "Do you really think the three of you can do something?"

"I do." Kimber sifted her fingers through the silky hair at his nape. "Except I don't think we should risk Maggie."

"Why not? You're a woman and we'd be risking you."

"She's pregnant. Maybe seven months or so." She didn't follow through with what would be a logical "I'm not" because, well, she was. And she didn't want to outright lie to Duncan. An omission wasn't exactly a falsehood, though she knew when he found out he wouldn't see it in quite the same way she did. "It's Jason's." She frowned. "Well, I think it is. I didn't ask."

"I don't suppose it matters," Duncan replied quietly. His gaze met hers. "I won't do anything that puts you at unnecessary risk," he said. "You mean too much to me."

"Even if we could stop the apocalypse?"

"Even then." He pressed a kiss to her brow. "I love you, Kimberly Treat, and I'm not giving you up. Not to zombies, not to the Unseen. We'll figure this out."

She saw the inner conflict on his face. If he did encourage her and she and the others were able to end the apocalypse, it was possible when everything was said and done he might lose her, too, because of the Unseen inside her. She fought the urge to blurt out her news. If he knew she was pregnant, he'd definitely put the kibosh on this plan of hers. She didn't want to risk her unborn child, but she needed to set things right in the world. She'd had a hand in starting this, even if it wasn't exactly

her fault. She needed to be the one to end it. She didn't want to
raise her child—any child, for that matter—in this zombieriffic
world.

* * *

Just when she thought she might see if she could do something
with the hard wedge of man flesh pressing against her hip, a
knock on the door came. When she tried hopping off Duncan's
lap, he tightened his hold. "Come," he barked.

The door swung open to reveal Atticus. He seemed startled,
and definitely not happy, to see Kimber there.

She pushed back the hurt she felt at his attitude. Since she
didn't know what to say at this point, she didn't say anything.

"Sorry," Atticus said with another glance at Kimber. "We're
scheduled for a meeting with Vachon. He's ready."

Duncan's arms loosened and Kimber climbed off his lap. As
he stood, a tall, muscular man strolled into the office. He wore
navy slacks with a crisp, long-sleeved white dress shirt. His dark
hair was caught at the nape of his neck with a leather band. Blue
eyes held intelligence and good humor.

Duncan shook the newcomer's hand. "I hope your stay so far
has been pleasant, Xavier."

"Your hospitality is most gracious," he said with a brief incline of his head. "And here is your very good friend Kimber."
His widening smile deepened the color of his eyes. "It's good to
see you again."

Kimber shot him a glance. "You, too," she said, but anger

began heating her inside. *Here we go with the 'very good friend' bullshit again.* What the hell?

Duncan cleared his throat. "Shall we get started, then? Kimber, I'll see you later."

She forced a smile. She didn't see any reason why she couldn't be in this meeting—why she *shouldn't* be in this meeting—but she wasn't going to press the issue in front of a stranger. "Of course." To Xavier she said, "I imagine we'll be seeing more of you. I'll let you get your meeting started." She went up on tiptoe and placed a kiss against Duncan's lips, then smiled at Atticus as she went by.

Atticus, who used to be her friend, didn't want to be in the same room with her anymore, and her lover called her a "very good friend." She sighed and closed the office door behind her. This had been the worst day ever.

Chapter Seven

By ten o'clock that night, Kimber was beat. She'd had no idea that being pregnant and stressed and worrying about what exactly her lover meant by *very good friend* could make a woman so fatigued. Tossing down the mystery novel she'd been reading, she heaved herself off the sofa and toddled toward the bedroom. Duncan was still with Xavier and Atticus and probably would be until the early hours of morning. Right now Kimber was too tired to even think about staying up to wait for Duncan. Maybe she'd take a nap with him later on. The way she was feeling right now, she thought a lot of naps might be in her future.

She took a quick shower and pulled on one of Duncan's soft T-shirts but didn't put on any panties. They made her uncomfortable while she slept. Crawling beneath the covers, she lay on her back and placed one hand over her abdomen. "Well, little one," she whispered, "I guess it's just you and me right now. I don't think your daddy meant to imply anything by calling me a very good friend. I mean, he could hardly call me his girlfriend, right? How silly would that be, an alpha vampire calling me his girlfriend, like we're teenagers? And it's not like he can call me his fiancée, either, since he hasn't asked me to marry him. And I'm not sure what I'd say if he did," she rambled on. "I think I'd say yes. I love him, so of course I'd say yes. Probably."

Kimber didn't understand why she felt so ambivalent. Any woman would jump at the chance to marry the man she loved, right? So why was she waffling?

Her thoughts continued to natter at her as she spiraled down into sleep.

* * *

The full moon lit the small city park, showing clearly the horde shuffling toward her. Kimber turned to run but stopped to see she was surrounded by zombies. She reached for the hatchet at her waist. Her fingers closed around air. What the hell? Why had she come outside and gone a mile and a half away from the compound without at least carrying some sort of weapon?

Her heart thrummed wildly in her chest. She looked around to find something—anything—she could use. Nothing. Not even a rock or a stick. Taking a deep breath, she looked for a break in the circle closing ever tighter around her. There! Another breath, and she took off like the hounds of hell were on her heels.

With only a little difficulty, she managed to push through the horde. She put on a burst of speed. Just as she reached the outer perimeter of the park, more zombies spilled out of the woods, trying to cut off her escape.

Then she saw the vampires, perched on overturned cars, standing on the curb across the street. Watching. Waiting.

Waiting for what?

"Help me!" she yelled.

"I told you I wouldn't jeopardize my people so you could play in the park." Duncan stepped forward from behind a line of beefy enforcers. "This was your choice, to put your life at risk. So you get to live with the consequences."

Live with the... Was he kidding? If he didn't help her, there wasn't going to be much more living being done by her. "Duncan, you can be mad at me later. Right now, I really could use your help." The last word came out as a screech as she dodged rotting hands reaching for her. On some level she was aware of how surreal this was, but she was too panicked to do much more than plead for help. "Please!"

He shook his head and folded his arms across his chest. Even though his face looked sad, his posture spoke to his in-tractability. "Sorry. I'd lose too many people trying to get you out of this mess. I'm afraid you're on your own, my very good friend."

As he turned away, she watched him in numb disbelief. Her lover, the father of her baby, was going to let her die, and the members of his vampire enclave weren't going to defy him. She was merely human, after all.

"I'm pregnant!" she screamed, her voice shrill and brit-tle. Her belly tightened. Her skin grew clammy and cold *even as her mouth went as dry as a desert. "You have to help me."*

He paused and turned around. "Damn you," he snarled with hands curled into fists. "How dare you risk my unborn child this way?"

She flinched at the rage in his tone. "I was trying to do the right thing." She jerked away from another zombie and gagged at the smell of decomposition permeating the air around her.

"Then call upon the Unseen," came his unsympathetic reply. "Save yourself. There's nothing I can do."

Then they were gone. Poof. Vanished between one blink and the next, leaving Kimber alone, surrounded by the walking dead.

She tried to tap into the Unseen within her and sobbed when all she found was emptiness. Despair rose inside her. Where was it? "It's here," she mewled. "I know it's here. It has to be here." All these months she'd been wanting to get rid of the Unseen squatting inside her, and now that she apparently had, she needed it.

Clutching hands bore her to the ground. The moonlight began to strobe, zombie faces appearing and disappearing with the blinking light. Teeth gnashed, eager to feed on her but never coming quite close enough to do so. This had to be a dream. If it were real life, she would've already felt them tearing at her flesh. But why couldn't she wake up?

A small burst of heat spread outward from her womb, filling her with warmth and the feeling of serenity, and just

enough confidence to burst through the nightmare holding
her in its dark grip.

* * *

Kimber shot upright with a gasp. The sense of well-being
slowly faded, as did the very real warmth coming from deep
inside her womb. Wonderingly, she placed her palms flat
against her belly. Had her baby helped her? Brought her to
enough alertness that she'd been able to wake from that too-
real nightmare?

"Thank you, little guy," she whispered, and rubbed circles
on her abdomen. A little flutter of awareness streaked through
her mind, making her gasp. Did her baby have a sort of mental
telepathy? If so, was it because of Kimber's necromancer abilities or Duncan's vampiric tendencies? Or a combination of the
two? While a vampire fathering a baby was rare, it wasn't impossible. It just took regular feeding and lots and lots of sex. So, for
her and Duncan, it had been actually rather easy for her to get
pregnant. She snorted a laugh and tried to ignore how close to
hysteria she felt.

Her heart pitter-pattered a crazy rhythm. Could the baby's
ability be because of the Unseen within her?

Oh, dear God. If her baby was tapped into the Unseen, what
would happen to him? She couldn't quite understand it, but
somehow she *knew* it was a boy. Could she protect him if she
managed to drive the Unseen back to itself?

Did she actually now *need* the Unseen to be part of her? Was that what her dream was trying to tell her? But what would that mean long-term? And how would she tell Duncan?

Crap. How was she going to tell Duncan she was pregnant? She knew he'd never react the way he had in the dream, never in a million years. He might not be willing to risk his people to save her and their baby, but he'd sure risk himself.

She got up and went into the bathroom for some water. As she brought the glass to her mouth, her hand shook and she ended up sloshing water up her nostrils. She grabbed a tissue and blew her nose, then drank down the rest of the water. Feeling calmer, she settled back into bed and let herself drift into sleep once again.

A while later she felt the mattress dip. Lips pressed against the curve of her neck. Duncan must be finished for the day, which meant the sun was up. Feeling nowhere near rested, she opened her eyes, blinking sleepily.

"Hey." He kissed her lips and stroked the hair at her temple. "I didn't mean to wake you."

"It's all right," she murmured, her voice raspy with sleep. Still shaken by the dream and the thoughts that still hadn't settled, she turned more fully into his embrace. "I had a bad dream, and I feel better now that you're here."

"Go back to sleep, sweetheart." He kissed the corner of her mouth. "I'll bring you up to speed after we've both gotten some rest."

Feeling more alert by the second, she decided she wanted to hear about their basic plans, at the very least. "Just give me the highlights."

"Xavier's really intelligent and a competent civil engineer. He has some good ideas for the construction of the corridor." He slanted his mouth over hers, getting her hot and bothered, then drew back with a grin. "Also, Atticus said he was going to talk to Natalie." His expression sobered. "I think he's going to release her from their agreement, now that Aodhán is back."

Kimber frowned. "But his agreement with Nat doesn't involve sex, so why should it matter?"

"Hmm. And how would you feel if I decided to feed from someone else, even if we weren't having sex?" He laughed at the little growl she let out and hugged her.

She wrapped her arms around his bare back to return the hug. At least he was touching her. And her libido perked up as she realized he was naked, which was his usual state when he went to bed. Maybe she could get him to do more than hug her now that she seemed to have caught a second wind.

"You know there's still a sexual element to feeding even if sex itself isn't involved."

"Okay, okay. I get it." She blinked, her eyes getting almost too heavy to keep open. So much for her second wind. "Atticus feeding from Natalie now that Aodhán is back is bad." She started to say more but was caught by a wide yawn.

Duncan pressed his mouth to her temple. "All right, that's enough for now. Let's get some sleep."

Kimber turned onto her side and snuggled against him, her rear settling against his groin. His body perked up in interest, and she wiggled again until his hand clamped down on her hip.

"Stop," he groaned. "We can get up to speed on this, too, after we've rested."

She grinned and closed her eyes. It was enough that he wanted her. After that dream, she needed all the assurance she could get.

* * *

Duncan stared down at the love of his life and felt the ache in his chest ease. Kimber was so fiercely independent and one of the strongest people, emotionally, he knew. He wasn't sure how much of that was from what she used to do for a living and how much of it came from being on her own. She had no family, not since her parents had been killed by vampires. It made him feel a bit primitive to think she needed him…for anything, but especially to make her feel more secure.

He'd made it his mission to protect her all those months ago, and he would never regret it, nor would he give her up. She was his to love, to protect.

And he was hers, even if it meant letting her use him for the zombie cure. If it came to that, he had little hope he would survive. But if he could make the world a safer place for Kimber, his death would be a small price to pay.

Chapter Eight

Natalie held up one hand, cutting Big Tom's tirade off mid-rant. "If you would just let me finish a sentence?" She waited until he clamped his lips together and gave a red-faced nod. His color wasn't due to embarrassment, she knew. He was royally pissed off. At least he wasn't swinging his fists. Yet.

"Until we can set up some sort of enclosed corridor, no one leaves the compound except scouting and raiding parties," she finished. "So the answer isn't an outright no. It's a wait. Please."

"Yeah. I'll believe it when I see it." He mumbled a few curses and turned away, a half-dozen men following behind and grousing under their breath.

"You know, Natalie, Tom doesn't speak for all of us," a man standing behind her said. "Most of us appreciate what we have here."

Before she could respond, Tom and his minions came barreling across the room. "You appreciate being a captive?" Tom shouted, getting in the guy's face. "You're nothing but a pansy-ass."

Natalie tried to move between the men, speaking in the most placating tone of voice she could. "Now, Tom—"

The big man shot her a glare. "You stay out of this, missy. Vampire lover," he snarled as he shoved her aside. His big fist shot out and slammed into the other man's face, sending him sprawling to the floor.

Then it was a free-for-all, and the only thing Natalie could do was try to stay out of everyone's way as the vampire guards waded in to break things up. When they got Tom settled into a chair, their sharp fangs and glares kept him in place. She went over to him. "Whatever else you may think, Duncan hasn't set rules in place arbitrarily. They're for our safety. All of us, human and vampire alike."

He snorted, then winced, gingerly touching his bleeding nose. "We're not allowed to go anywhere without an escort. How is that fair?"

"And other than Duncan, Atticus, and the guards assigned to this area, no other vampires are allowed down here. Tell me how that's not fair."

She got nowhere with the hardheaded jerk, finally throwing up her hands in defeat and leaving. As she made her way to her room, Natalie heaved a sigh of relief. Twenty minutes later, she finished writing her report and set the legal tablet aside on the coffee table. Even after all these months it still felt weird to handwrite something that before the Outbreak would have been done on a computer. Her report detailed this latest run-in with Big Tom. She'd wanted to get her thoughts down on paper before she forgot some of the more subtle nuances of the altercation. In her opinion, it hadn't been serious enough to bother Duncan with right away, so she'd decided to wait until this evening to update him on the situation.

She was half tempted to advise him to kick Big Tom and his cronies out, but then what? They'd be nothing more than zombie bait. They'd never last out there. More and more she tried to put herself in their shoes and knew if she were stuck downstairs without getting to see the sun or sky, she'd probably start going a little stir-crazy, too.

Maybe that's why she'd been more conciliatory than she had at their last meeting, because Big Tom, while he'd been his normal belligerent, obnoxious self as he'd spouted off about making deals with a bunch of devils, hadn't tried to hit her this time. She had a feeling if he had, Atticus wouldn't have let it go a second time. He'd been coldly furious when he'd learned that Big Tom had hit her a couple of weeks ago, going even stiffer with rage as the bruise on her face had shown in black and deep purple with shades of blue. Now it was a mottled green and yellow that she could mostly cover up with foundation.

Nevertheless, Atticus usually took a close look at her cheek whenever they got together for her weekly donation of blood to him. She closed her fingers around her forearm, thinking of the carnal pain caused by his bite and the suction of his mouth as he fed, the way he made the pain fade into sensual pleasure so great she almost had an orgasm every time.

A knock came at her door. She rose to her feet and padded barefoot to the door. A quick peek through the peephole brought Atticus into view. Speak of the devil. Or one of them, anyway.

She opened the door. He stood there, feet braced slightly apart. Big, broad, and sexy. In a moment when she'd felt so alone, so abandoned, she'd thought about deepening their relationship, but that idea had evaporated like rainwater in the desert as soon as Aodhán had come back. "I thought you'd be in bed already." She stood back to let Atticus into her apartment. "Can I get you anything?" she asked. *Coffee, tea, me?* She bit back a giggle and wiped her hands on the thighs of her jeans. She wasn't sure why she was so nervous. It was only Atticus, after all. But there was a look in those silver eyes of his that told her she might not like what he'd come to say.

After he took her chin in his fingers and tilted her head to get a better look at the fading bruises on her face, he gave a satisfied nod and released her. "Let's sit down," he said, and motioned toward the sofa in the small living room.

She took a seat and waited for him to speak. When he sat beside her and stared at his hands, clasped between his spread knees, she couldn't stand it any longer. "What's going on?" She stared at him, her pulse picking up speed. She'd never seen this self-possessed man seem so hesitant before.

He looked up, and she gasped at the misery written in the lines of his face. He shifted to face her and took her hands in his. With his thumbs sweeping gently across her knuckles, he murmured, "I know how you feel about Aodhán." When she opened her mouth, he tightened his fingers and gave her that look that meant *Shut up and let me talk*. "I've always known, but I took advantage of his absence and persuaded you into our agreement."

"You didn't take advantage of me, Atticus," she assured him. "I wanted to help you."

He nodded. "You have a kind, generous heart, Natalie." His thumbs started stroking her knuckles again. "And it belongs to Aodhán. So I release you from our agreement."

For once everything this taciturn vampire felt was clear to see in his eyes, on his drawn face. He looked sad. Heartbroken.

Dear. God. He was in love with her. How had she missed that?

"Atticus..."

He squeezed her hands gently, released them, and got to his feet. When she stood, he cupped her face in his big hands, dropping his mouth to hers in a brief kiss. "Be with Aodhán without guilt, Natalie," he said, his voice raspy and quiet. "My life is the richer for your friendship, which we will always have. But if he makes you unhappy," he added in a tone as hard as steel, "he will answer to me." He stepped back.

"Wait." She grabbed his wrist, knowing she held him in place only because he allowed it. "You haven't fed all week." She shoved out her arm, soft side up. "Please."

His lips firmed. "I don't like pity feeds any more than I like pity fucks."

She frowned. "I wasn't...that wasn't what I...," she huffed. "I'm worried about you, you big lug. It'll probably take a couple of days for you to make an arrangement with another donor, and you need to feed sooner rather than later." When he didn't move, she dropped her arm to her side. "Fine. Just don't come whining to me when the hunger really gets bad."

He scooped up her arm and held it gently in his hands. Silver eyes gleaming, he licked his lips. "I admit my control will not be what it should be if I don't feed soon." He stared into her face. "I won't make this pleasurable for you, Natalie. It would be too much like cheating. I can dull the pain of my bite somewhat, but you will still feel it."

She swallowed. While he'd been so gentle with her, it had been easy to forget he was an apex predator and she was weak, puny prey. She trusted him, though, not to hurt her beyond the pain of the bite. She squeezed her eyes shut and turned her head away. "Go ahead."

Natalie heard his deep chuckle, then felt the cool brush of his fangs against her arm before they pierced her skin. Her eyes shot open, and she couldn't hold back a squall of pain. She sucked in a breath and panted. God. If this was him blunting the pain, she'd hate to know what a full-on bite without any vampire glamour felt like. After a few seconds, his mouth lifted and his tongue stroked over her skin, sealing the wound. In an hour there wouldn't be any sign at all that he'd fed from her.

That made her inexplicably sad.

His hand came up to her face, his thumb swiping away a tear she'd been unaware of shedding. She saw the same misery she felt reflected in his eyes.

"I don't know why I'm crying," she said on a sob.

Atticus drew her into his arms, pressing her head against his chest. "It is a natural reaction to the end of a blood-consort relationship," he said. "This sadness you feel will pass. Don't fight it. Just breathe and have faith that all will unfold as it should."

She pulled away and swiped her hands across her cheeks. "I'll find you a match as soon as possible."

"I have no doubt you will." He touched the tips of his fingers to her cheek, then turned away. He paused at the open door. "Thank you, Natalie." Then he was gone, the door closing behind him.

She slumped back onto the sofa. Still the tears crept down her face. She couldn't shut them off. Through watery vision, she watched the round wounds on her inner forearm close. Close to an hour after Atticus had left, there were only two red spots where his fangs had thrust through her skin. She lightly rubbed at them and wondered if she was crazy for wishing they'd scarred so that she'd have a visual reminder of her time with him.

Someone knocked, and her first thought was that Atticus had come back to tell her he'd changed his mind, that he wanted to stay with her. That he wanted to have more. Because at least Atticus was a sure thing. She knew she could count on him to be there for her. He wanted her, and not just because her blood tasted good. And while she might not have the same feelings for him as she did for Aodhán, at least she wouldn't be alone when she died. With Aodhán, she just wasn't sure how long he'd stay. He was, after all, not of this realm and had obligations elsewhere. But Atticus, on the other hand…She raced to the door and threw it open.

Aodhán stood here, his handsome mouth curved in a smile. "Hello, *mo chroí.*"

Wordlessly she waved him inside. She didn't understand the

disappointment she felt that he wasn't her Roman vampire. She loved Aodhán and she was happy to see him, but at the same time she had this deep longing for Atticus.

She was so confused.

Aodhán pulled her into a loose embrace. "What is it? What's wrong?"

How could she tell the man she loved that she was pining for another?

"If it helps, Atticus came to see me." Aodhán ran his broad hands up and down her back, slow, heated strokes that comforted and brought the tingling beginnings of arousal at the same time. "He told me what you'd be feeling. It's okay."

Natalie stared up at him. In what world could it possibly be okay? Oh, right. In a world of a zombie apocalypse, where up was down and wrong was right. "You're sure?" she asked. "'Cause if the situation were reversed, I'm not so certain I'd be as magnanimous."

He brushed a kiss across her lips. "Did you fall in love with him?" His eyes held hers.

She shook her head. "No. He's a friend, that's all."

"Then it's okay."

She searched his features and saw only love and acceptance. With a sigh she leaned into him, resting her cheek against his hard chest. Amazingly, her yearnings for the vampire began to fade as a fire of a different sort began burning. She lifted her head and looked into his face, licking her suddenly dry lips.

With a low groan, he bent his head and set his mouth on hers. The feel of his firm yet soft lips was as arousing as the first time he'd kissed her. She moaned into his mouth and closed her eyes, pressing closer against him, moving her mouth under his, parting her lips for the sweep of his tongue into her mouth. He tasted so good, so *right*.

His lips left hers to explore her jaw, the slope of her neck, the hollow of her throat. She shifted, sliding her hands over his back, slowly rocking her hips against his, feeling his cock harden against her belly. His muscles tensed, his hands tightening at her waist, pulling her even closer. He went back to her lips and plundered them as if determined to make a meal of her mouth.

Natalie moaned and tangled her fingers in Aodhán's hair, moving her lips against his, thrusting her tongue into his mouth, demanding more. After a few minutes he gentled and rested his forehead against hers. His chest rose and fell heavily, and once his breathing had settled, he said, "You're addictive, you know that? I don't think I'll ever get enough of you." He adjusted his stance and dropped his mouth onto hers again.

He slid his arms around her, one at her waist and the other tugging her hips closer. She tilted her head into his kiss and arched her back to press her breasts against his chest. When a low groan, almost a growl, came from his throat, she lifted one leg and wrapped it around his narrow hip, pressing her jeans-covered sex against his hardening groin. He stroked his hand from her hip to her ass, cupping her, holding her tightly to him.

Her belly tightened, her core clenching with need. With another growling groan, Aodhán scooped her up and placed her gently on the sofa. He stroked long, elegant fingers down her cheek. "I need to taste you, *mo chroí*, need to lick your sweet honey. Will you let me?"

Her breath caught in her throat. No man had ever asked permission to go down on her before. Not that she had all that much experience, but the little she did have had been of the *stick a tongue in, swirl it around a little, and call it good* variety, and it had only been so the man could say he'd given her foreplay before he did what he really was focused on, which was getting his cock some action. She somehow knew that Aodhán was different, that his only thought was focused on her. At the thought of him putting his mouth, his tongue, on her there…Slick heat bloomed in the folds between her thighs. "Oh, God, Aodhán." She traced a finger over his jaw and lingered on his full bottom lip. "Please."

His clear blue eyes darkened with passion. "May I undress you?" At her nod, he gently removed her shoes and socks, his fingers lingering a moment on her feet before he lifted her torso and pulled her shirt over her head. He paused, his hands on her shoulders, as he looked down at her breasts, the upper slopes bared by her leopard-print demi-bra.

Her face went hot. "Just because it's a zombie apocalypse doesn't mean a woman can't wear sexy underwear," she muttered.

A grin flashed over his face. "I like it very much, *mo chroí*. I stopped to admire the view." He worked the front clasp loose and gently pushed the cups aside. "Beautiful," he whispered. "Like a work of art." He pressed her back against the cushions of the sofa and brought his mouth to her breast. She felt the swipe of his tongue as he drew one nipple to a hard point, then the other. "I'll spend time here later," he promised in a low, dark voice. "But I need to taste you now. I want to feel you come on my mouth."

His strong hands went to the button on her jeans. He flipped it open, then carefully slid her zipper down. She lifted her hips and let him tug off her jeans and panties.

With his gaze zeroed in on her feminine flesh, a muscle leaped in his jaw and his nostrils flared. "I can smell your arousal," he murmured, and dipped his head closer. He lifted her left leg so it rested against the back of the sofa and draped her right leg over his shoulder. He placed one hand just below her belly button and with the other spread the swollen lips of her sex. His hot tongue quickly followed.

As he flicked his tongue against her clit, her head fell back and she moaned. "Oh, God, Aodhán. That feels so good."

He shifted his weight, wedging her thighs farther apart with his broad shoulders, like he was getting comfortable, like he planned to stay right where he was for a while. His tongue slid down to stroke inside her sheath a few moments before going back to her clit where his lapping became much more purposeful. He suckled her clit gently at first, then with harder suction. Carnal delight shivered up her spine. When he slipped one thick finger inside her, she flexed her hips, helpless to stop the reflexive motion.

His movements were slow and steady, teasing her, taunting her with what was to come. He added another finger and twisted his hand so it was palm up. Still sucking on her clit, he strummed his fingers back and forth, building a wild pressure. She gasped and moaned as the sensation increased, the tension in her body building to an unbearable tightness. Yet the wave of pleasure kept rising.

"You're so tight on my fingers, *mo chroí*. So wet and hot." He crooked his fingers in a come-hither motion, rubbing against that spot that made her legs jerk in reaction. "Come for me, Natalie," he urged.

Like a rubber band breaking after being stretched too taut, her body found sweet release and she came in a tidal wave of wanton bliss. She screamed and his fingers continued to stroke as she came in a slick tide of completion.

His tongue replaced his fingers and he lapped at her juices. With each lingering pulse of her orgasm, her hips flexed against his mouth, driving his tongue deeper. She tried to catch her breath, shuddering on an aftershock when he slid his tongue into her pussy one last time.

She'd had no idea the lengths to which a man like Aodhán would go to please a woman. To please her. She could have had this with him for the last six months or so. Why had she fought her attraction so hard?

"I love you," he said, his cheek pressed against her mound.

She glanced down and saw his erection pressing against the placket of his leather pants. She struggled to sit up, frowning when he put a big hand on her chest and kept her in place. "Aodhán, let me return the favor."

He shook her head, his face moving against her skin. "Not necessary. This was all about you. For you." His eyes closed and he drew in a deep breath. "Just let me stay here for a bit. I've finally come home."

Natalie bit her lip and fought back tears. She'd seen Aodhán fierce, playful, irreverent, and now gentle and so sweet she wanted to wrap herself around him and never let go.

Maybe there was a future for them, after all.

Or…maybe not. Maybe there really wasn't a future for any of them.

Chapter Nine

Kimber came awake slowly to the sensation of a warm, wet tongue stroking between the folds of her sex and strong fingers tugging and pinching her hardened nipples beneath the soft T-shirt she wore. She moaned and spread her legs farther apart. "What a hell of a way to wake up," she whispered, reaching down to tangle her fingers in Duncan's silky hair. She glanced toward the window and realized night had fallen, as there was very little light coming in from around the curtains. Several candles burned on the bedside table, making her wonder just how long he'd been awake. Long enough to get her motor revving, that was for sure.

That was the best sleep she'd had in a week, and she knew it was because Duncan had been with her, his body against hers, while they'd rested.

"It came to me, as I lay here watching you sleep, that I've been neglectful this past week." He pressed his lips to her inner thigh. "I'd like to say it had nothing to do with what you did to Atticus, but I'd be lying." His shoulders bunched with tension. "Couple that with the elevated aggression that seems to be riding you…" He trailed off and kissed her thigh again. "I'm sorry, baby. It wasn't well done of me." Regret colored his deep tones.

Her heart eased. She'd been so afraid that he'd been pulling away from her. Maybe he had, but at least he'd recognized it and had realized what he was doing. She sifted his hair through her fingers. "I promise you, I will never deliberately hurt you. And I'll do my best to not let what happened to Atticus happen to anyone else. You have my word." She gave a light tug on his hair. "Now come up here and kiss me."

"And here I thought I *was* kissing you." His lips moved up her thigh to pause next to her mound.

"My lips. Kiss my lips." And before he could say the smart-ass thing she knew he was going to, she added a little testily, "The lips on my face, fang boy."

His deep chuckle rolled over her, delighting her with his playfulness. But when he lifted his head and she saw the green of his irises shot through with vampire silver, glittering in the candlelight, her core rippled with renewed heat. "Come up here," she insisted, her entire body catching fire for him.

"By your command." He came up over her, muscles bunching and flexing. When he slanted his lips over hers, she tasted her own essence and it ratcheted her arousal up another notch. His tongue swept inside her mouth to duel with hers, twining, sliding, rubbing.

"I want you inside me," she moaned. Curling her legs around

his hips, she reached down and grasped his erection to position it at the entrance to her channel.

His breath hissed between his teeth. "God, I love your hands on me." He broke her hold on him long enough to sweep the T-shirt over her head, letting it drop to the floor beside the bed. As her hand went back to his cock, he rocked his hips forward and slid the head inside her opening. "You're so beautiful," he whispered, his eyes dark with passion but full of love. He draped one of her legs over a brawny forearm, bracing his weight with his palm flat against the mattress, and pressed the palm of his other hand against her mound just above her clit. He pushed into her, his jaw tense. "You're so tight, so hot, it's going to kill me someday." He dipped his head and kissed her. "But what a way to go."

Kimber clutched his heavy biceps. His cock was hard and yet silky, filling her so completely with his thickness. "Give it to me," she demanded, tightening her grip on his arms.

Duncan looked down, still holding her thigh over his right forearm. He ran a fingertip through her slick folds and slid it over her clit before beginning to rock his hips in a slow, sensuous rhythm, feeding more and more of his cock into her sheath until his balls finally slapped against the curve of her buttocks. He paused, his face dark and taut. "Are you all right?"

"Better than all right," she assured him. Then she frowned. "But I won't be for long if you don't start moving, mister."

His grin delighted her soul. "Yes, ma'am." He let her leg fall to the bed and grasped her hips. He tilted her to him in a way that created an amazing friction on her clit and hit that sensitive spot inside her that made her moan every time his cock slid over it. Dear. God. In. Heaven. "Harder!" she cried. Her arousal spiraled ever tighter, taking her higher and higher, closer and closer to a free fall.

He pulled back and thrust in, harder and faster with every stroke. Every muscle in her body tensed, her back bowed as his hips pistoned back and forth. When he moved one hand between their bodies and rubbed her clit, she flew apart, the tension in her body shattering into a million pieces. She screamed as she came, barely aware of his final thrust and his deep voice joining hers in a shout as he found his own release. He held her tightly to him and ground his hips against hers, sending her into a wave of aftershocks, and all she could do was gasp and moan and hold on to him when he leaned down and fit his fangs to her throat.

The tug of his mouth on her skin as he drank from her neck brought on another orgasm, not as strong as the first one but just as powerful emotionally. She felt his tongue lick over her wounds; then he rested his face against her shoulder.

As the sensual storm passed, she tried to catch her breath. She curled her hands around his nape, running her fingers through his hair. He rose up to look down at her. His face was relaxed, his eyes once again a normal green. "I love you," he whispered, and pressed his lips to the corner of her mouth. Muscles bunched as he gathered her in his arms and rolled them over so she was on top, their intimate connection unbroken.

"I love you, too. So much." Still breathing hard, she laid her head on his shoulder and stroked her fingers through the smattering of dark hair on his chest. His hand smoothed over her head in a gesture so tender it brought a rush of tears to her eyes. Damn pregnancy hormones. After a few seconds, she asked, "Duncan?"

"Hmmm?"

She licked her lips. "Why did you introduce me to Xavier as your very good friend?"

He shifted his weight beneath her but his arms didn't loosen, holding her against him. "I didn't know what else to say. Girlfriend seems inadequate and even juvenile, and lover makes it sound like you're my mistress, and that's not how I see you at all." His shrug moved her cheek up and down. "So I went with very good friend."

"Oh." She thought it over and understood his reasoning. Of course, if he'd just ask her to marry him, he could introduce her as his fiancée. But maybe he wasn't ready to take that step yet. She certainly wasn't brazen enough to ask him. There were many things she was brave enough to do—kill zombies and fight vampires without a moment's hesitation. But ask a man to marry her? No way.

What if he said no?

They lay like that in silence for several minutes, Duncan continuing to brush his hands up and down her back. "This is nice," he finally said, his voice soft in the stillness of the room. He lifted his hips, driving his softening cock into her heat. "I could stay like this forever."

"Wouldn't get much work done." She closed her eyes on a satiated but sleepy sigh.

His low chuckle caused his chest to reverberate against her.

"No, I suppose we wouldn't." His hands kept moving, stroking her skin, leaving tingling awareness in their wake. "I'm sorry I was so distant this week, sweetheart. More sorry than I can say."

She tilted her head up to look at him. "Apology accepted. Now let's forget about it. Life's too short. We're here together now, loving each other, so there can't be any regrets." She pressed her lips to his chest, feeling the hardness of muscle beneath hair-roughened skin. "I love you."

She felt the touch of his mouth on the top of her head. "There's no one else for me but you, Kimber. You captured my heart the moment we met." Another chuckle moved the chest beneath her. "Though you did lead me on quite the chase."

"Only until you caught me."

"Hmm." He tilted her chin and kissed her lips. It was a sweet kiss, one full of affection. It moved her as much as his passion had.

She felt tears start again and ducked her chin to rest her head against his shoulder. She knew she would love this man forever. Like him, she'd be content to lie here like this with him until the end of time.

Except her stomach had other ideas.

Out of nowhere came a roll of nausea so potent Kimber jerked upright. Her eyes wide against the urge, she vaulted out of the bed and barely made it to the bathroom in time. As she hung over the toilet and prayed for death, she became aware of Duncan kneeling behind her, holding her hair away from her face, one big hand smoothing up and down her back. Just when she thought she was finished, another wave hit her. Her back bowed and she gripped the rounded edge of the bowl.

She flushed and rested there a minute, just to be sure. When she started to gather her feet beneath her, he put his hand under her elbow and helped her up. She rinsed out her mouth and brushed her teeth for good measure. The worst of the nausea seemed to have passed, though her stomach still felt a little unsettled.

"Are you all right?" Duncan stood behind her, one hand outstretched as if he were ready to support her if she needed it.

Tell him, her conscience prodded. "Must have been something I ate," she said with a shrug. When she told him about the baby, she didn't want it to be right after she'd practically chucked up a lung in front of him. She wanted to be more in control, feel even a little bit sexy, not like a squeezed, worn-out dishrag.

She took a shaky step toward the bedroom. With a soft curse, he swept her into his arms and carried her back to bed. Once she was settled between the sheets, he sat down beside her. "Why don't you rest a while longer?" he suggested, brushing her hair away from her forehead. He cupped her cheek and brushed his thumb over her lower lip. "I've been thinking about your proposition with the practice zombies, and I'd like to talk with you and the other necromancers more about it. Do you think you'll be up to meeting in two hours?"

"Of course." She sat up against the headboard and clutched the sheet over her breasts. It was more than being self-conscious about him seeing her naked breasts. Already with the pregnancy they were changing, becoming fuller, the nipples larger and more sensitive. She didn't want him finding out about the baby by guessing, but she'd tell him when she was ready. And she wasn't ready yet.

It was like she had a Good Kimber and a Naughty Kimber riding on her shoulders, one adamant that she should tell him and one equally opposed. And right now, she was going to listen to Naughty Kimber.

He leaned forward and placed a chaste kiss on her lips. "I'll let you know the specific time. Get some more sleep." He got up and went back into the bathroom, and within a few seconds she heard the shower start up. She slid down in bed and turned on her side. Hugging his pillow, she closed her eyes. Maybe she'd doze for a few more minutes.

* * *

Duncan toweled himself dry and swiped another towel over his hair, then ran his fingers through the damp strands. Going back into the bedroom naked, he smiled to see Kimber sound asleep, holding his pillow against her chest, her right leg drawn up, allowing him to see the soft folds of her sex.

He eased down onto the bed and touched Kimber's hair ever so lightly. He'd been such an ass this past week, holding himself back from her. The first jolt of trepidation upon hearing what she'd done to Atticus was understandable, even forgivable. But for him to carry on as if she couldn't be trusted to touch him had been overreaction, pure and simple. She'd touched him plenty the day before she'd siphoned energy off of Atticus. It had been unintentional on her part and he'd been unwilling, or maybe even unable, to accept that.

All he'd been able to think of was what a danger she and others like her were to vampires. And while he'd been going on about protecting his "people," he'd almost alienated the woman he loved. She was his "people," too, and he'd be damned if he'd allow any situation to force him to choose between her or the vampires under his protection. The vamps would lose, hands down, every time.

He knew Atticus was still unnerved by what had happened, though he covered it up by being angry about it. The big vampire needed to let it go now. Duncan needed Atticus and Kimber working together, not skirting each other—and in Atticus's case, pretty much snarling every time she came near.

He stared down at his lover. She seemed to be sleeping peacefully, for which he was glad. He hated seeing her unwell, and thinking about her sickness rattled him more than anything else could. This was something he couldn't fix for her. He touched her hair again. He hoped she was right in thinking it was something she'd eaten. If it were more serious than that...

Hell. He scrubbed his hand over his face. They needed a doctor on-site. He should have seen to that right away, as soon as they'd started taking in humans. With their innate healing abilities, vampires really didn't need physicians, but humans certainly did. Another item to add to his ever-expanding list of things to do.

He leaned down and pressed a kiss to the corner of her

mouth. Her lips twitched into a soft smile and she mumbled something so indistinct even his preternatural hearing couldn't make out the exact words. She was adorable when she was like this, though he wasn't sure he'd ever tell her that. He liked his balls right where they were, thank you very much.

Chapter Ten

Duncan sat behind his desk and studied Natalie's handwritten report in front of him. With a scowl, he reread one particular paragraph: *Big Tom keeps pushing for humans to be taken to the park for exercise, only now he's also insisting it be once a day instead of three times a week as he'd asked before. In my opinion, his animosity toward vampires has increased, and I believe he's looking for an excuse to start something. One of the last things he told me before I ended our meeting was "Sometimes a situation becomes so intolerable the only avenue left open is a good, old-fashioned revolt."*

Duncan scrubbed his hand over his jaw. If someone had told him how much damn time he'd spend behind a desk, he might have rethought his plan to kill the former enclave leader. Maybe he'd been too hasty in castigating Maddalene for her heavy-handed way of running things. Some people—vampires and humans alike—seemed to only understand the way of the world when it was explained through violent means. Maybe if he bent

Big Tom over his arm and sank his fangs into the man's neck, he'd finally get just who and *what* he was pissing off with his ridiculous demands.

It appeared he had two tasks taking precedence right now. First up was to find a doctor for Kimber and the other humans, and second was to nip Big Tom's insolence in the bud. Because things were still so volatile from the change in leadership, Duncan couldn't leave the compound for the length of time it might take to find a physician. By default, that meant it was up to him to deal with the rabble-rouser. He'd send Atticus and his team out for a doc.

As if his thoughts had summoned him, his second-in-command poked his head through the open doorway. "Got a minute?" Atticus asked.

Duncan motioned him in with a wave of his hand.

The other vampire sauntered into the room and settled into one of the leather armchairs in front of Duncan's desk. "Any updates?" he asked.

To Duncan's way of thinking, that attitude was one of the reasons Atticus made such a great right hand. He never waited to be called by his boss; he made it a point to check in regularly. Duncan knew part of it was that he liked to keep busy, and being stuck inside was a surefire way to drive anyone crazy. His lips tightened and he pushed back a fledgling surge of empathy for Big Tom and his cohorts. Their situation was entirely different. Atticus and his team could go out and have a good chance of surviving among zombies, but with the way the hordes seemed to be congregating together, Tom and the others would be slaughtered within a mile. Duncan knew the big human disagreed with him and thought as long as they had weapons they could protect themselves, but Duncan had seen how quickly a zombie horde could overtake a group of people, and he still was not willing to risk any vampires to provide an escort.

He blew out an aggrieved sigh.

"Man, now I know something's up if you're doing that."

"Doing what?" He frowned.

"Sighing." Atticus crossed his legs and curled his fingers over the ends of the arms of his chair. "What's going on?"

Duncan hesitated while he pondered which situation to bring to Atticus's attention first. He decided to go with Big Tom even though he knew Atticus had about as much patience for the guy as he did. He'd break the news about wanting him to locate and bring back a doctor for Kimber afterward. Worse news following bad news.

Duncan tapped his index finger on the paper in front of him. "Natalie thinks Big Tom and his cronies may be gearing up for a rebellion. I keep thinking we should just open the gates and tell them whoever doesn't want to stay is free to leave."

"And the problem with that would be…"

"They'd probably be slaughtered within sight of the compound." The office chair creaked as Duncan leaned back. "That wouldn't do the morale of the remaining humans any good."

"Hmm. I suppose you're right on that." Atticus scratched his chin. "So you want me to go set Tom straight?"

Duncan pursed his lips. "Actually, no. I have another job for you, one outside the compound and I don't know how long it might take."

Atticus's dark brows dipped. "Just what the hell do you want from me?"

Duncan told him how Kimber had been sick earlier. "And it struck me that we don't have a physician here. If any of the humans get sick, we have no one who can care for them."

Atticus's jaw firmed. "Let me guess. You want me to go find a doctor for your girlfriend." He gave a soft snort of disgust. "Really, we need a doctor to protect everyone else from Kimber."

"That's enough." Duncan stood and leaned forward, bracing his weight with his palms flat on his desk. He wouldn't allow his friend to disrespect the woman he loved, no matter how much the other vampire might feel it was deserved. "Look, I get that she hurt you. She didn't do it on purpose—even you admitted to that. So why are you holding so hard on to this animosity of yours?"

Atticus stood, too, and began to pace in front of the desk, going from the outer wall to the inner one and back again. Duncan could see by the struggle on his face that his old friend searched for the right words to explain what he was feeling. Finally, his second-in-command said in a low voice, "I've never had anyone take me down like that, Duncan." His silvered gaze met Duncan's. "It's not an experience I want to repeat. She…rattled me."

"I get that. I do." Duncan came around and leaned one hip against the front of his desk. He folded his arms across his chest.

"You deal with this however you need to, as long as you stop disrespecting her and glaring at her whenever she comes near. She feels badly about it, you know."

Atticus gave an abrupt nod and came to a stop in front of him. "But if she can do something like that on her own, what do you think three of them together could do?"

That was the million-dollar question. But he had to trust her at some point, or how much was his love worth? "That's why I have guards on all of them, including Kimber."

"I'll put together a team and we'll head out tomorrow at dusk." A grin twitched at the corner of Atticus's mouth. "I guess that means you'll be handling Big Tom and his buddies?"

"Not that I want to, but he's not going to respect anyone with lesser authority." Duncan clapped a hand on his friend's shoulder. "You've got the easier job of it, I think. Someone gets in your way, all you have to do is chop off their head. Much as I might like to do that to Big Tom, I can't." He moved back around behind his desk and checked the time on the wind-up carriage clock on his desk. Calling out to one of the guards by the door, he asked him, "Please find Kimber and ask her and the other necromancers to come to my office."

The vampire acknowledged the order with a crisp nod and hurried away.

***

When Kimber led the other two necromancers into his office several minutes later, she was the only one who seemed confident. The other two appeared to be scared shitless. As the guard closed the door behind them, Kimber breezed right up to Duncan and planted a kiss on his mouth. As she stepped back, he looked her over. Her face was still a little pale but otherwise she was as beautiful as ever. "How are you feeling?" he asked quietly, stroking his fingers down her satiny cheek.

"I'm fine." She kissed him again and then moved around to the front of the desk. She perched on the edge so she could look at him as well as Maggie and Jason, who'd taken seats in the two leather armchairs in front of the desk. Atticus stood by the window where the two sitting in the armchairs would have to turn their heads to talk to him. Kimber stared at him a moment, then said, "Atticus." Her tone, full of regret and uncertainty on how to proceed, bespoke of the rift in their friendship.

He didn't move for a few seconds; then he dropped his hands to his sides and walked over to her. He stared down into her face before lifting one hand to softly brush her chin with his knuckles. "We're good, Kimber," he said. Leaning closer so that only she and Duncan could hear her, he added, "But if you ever do that to me again, our friendship will not save you."

"I understand."

Atticus shot Duncan a look as if daring him to take exception to his threat. Duncan held his gaze, knowing that if it ever came down to Atticus or Kimber, Duncan would back Kimber any day of the week. He let that knowledge sit in his eyes, and after his friend tipped his chin down, he knew the message had been received.

Kimber made the introductions and Atticus took his spot by the window again.

Duncan saw how the necromancers looked across the desk at him with a combination of trepidation and awe. "Am I the first vampire you've been this close to?" he asked.

"Well, no," Jason said. "But you're the king, right? That's a bit…" He sighed. "Intimidating." It was clear he didn't like making that public knowledge. As if Duncan couldn't sense his emotions anyway.

"As long as you follow the rules, you have nothing to fear here," Duncan assured him. "As I'm sure Natalie has explained to you."

"Oh, yes," Maggie rushed to say. "She's been great." She faltered and looked down at her hands clasped in her lap. Apparently Jason wasn't the only one a bit put off by him.

Kimber glanced toward the door, then looked at Duncan. "Shouldn't Brigid be here, too?"

"I'd prefer as few people as possible right now, until we know more. If I decide to allow you to move forward, then we'll bring her into it." He leaned back in his chair and stared at Kimber. "So, tell us this plan." He kept his gaze on her as she explained what she wanted to do.

"I want to capture at least three zombies and chain them up so it's safe for us to touch them. We'll have at least a dozen other zombies in a separate enclosure so we can use our mojo on them and see if we can put them down."

Maggie squirmed in her chair, drawing his attention.

"Are you all right?" he asked.

She nodded, then shook her head. "I'm sorry." She rubbed her swollen belly. "I should be done with morning sickness, but sometimes nausea hits me at the oddest times."

Kimber glanced at him. "Wastebasket," she mouthed.

He scooted his chair back and pulled the metal bin out from beneath his desk. She handed it over to Maggie, who gave a shaky "Thank you."

"No problem." Kimber pointed to the door behind Duncan's desk. "But there's a bathroom, if you need to, you know, and you have enough time to get in there."

Maggie gave her a smile and a soft, "Hopefully I won't need to."

"What do the two of you think of this plan?" Duncan asked after a moment, his gaze going from Maggie to Jason. "Are you certain you can pull it off?"

"I don't know if any other necromancers have ever tried to combine their powers before. I never have, so, no, I'm not certain of anything," Jason said. "But if it can stop the insanity, I'm all for trying."

"Maggie?" Duncan prompted.

Clutching the wastebasket to her chest, she swallowed. "I'm willing to try, but"—she looked at Kimber—"you said it might be bad for my baby."

"I can only tell you that it was a tremendous strain on my body," Kimber said. "You're already under stress just by virtue of being pregnant. But it's your decision."

Maggie nodded. "If you think it could work, I want to give it a try." She paled and swallowed rapidly.

Duncan glanced at Kimber and was surprised to see a funny look on her face, an almost…guilty expression. Now, why would she look at Maggie and feel guilty? When Kimber's eyes slid to his and the guilt deepened, he straightened abruptly. The way Maggie looked right now was the way Kimber had looked earlier, right before she'd puked her guts out. Without taking his gaze from his lover, he said, "Jason, Maggie, Atticus, would you please excuse us?" When the door closed behind them, he leaned back in his chair. "You have something you need to tell me, sweetheart?"

Her mouth opened, closed, opened again. Closed again. She swallowed. "Um…ah…" Her lips pressed together. "I was getting around to telling you," she whispered.

"Telling me what, exactly?"

She jumped off his desk and faced him fully. "I'm pregnant."

If his heart could beat, he knew it would stop with the shock of what she'd just told him. Shock gave way to joy that became muted by the misery he saw in her face. That a vampire could get a human pregnant was as close to a miracle as they could get. He wanted to shout his delight to the world, wanted to find a bunch of cigars and start handing them out. He and Kimber were going to have a baby! But she didn't seem to share his elation. He stared at her and wondered if he imagined that she was a little thicker, that her breasts were already a little bigger. A primitive caveman inside of him beat his chest with pride. He'd given his woman a baby, a little copy of the best of both of them. "You're not happy about this," he stated, beginning to feel miserable himself.

"The timing could be better." She threw out one hand and paced in front of his desk. "I'm having a baby in the middle of the zombie apocalypse, Duncan. *And* I have a piece of the Unseen inside me." She stopped, her eyes misty as she met his gaze. "What if that does something to the baby?"

He didn't like the sound of that at all. He went to her and drew her into his arms. "Is that possible?"

"I don't know!" she wailed. She jerked away from him and walked over to the window. "It's not like anyone's ever had the Unseen inside them before. Not that I know of, anyway. At any rate, it's not like there are any alternatives here," she said with her back to him.

He went still. The only alternative he knew to having a baby was to *not* have a baby. "You don't want it?" he asked, his voice raspy with pain.

She whirled to face him. "Oh, honey." She rushed over to him and threw her arms around his waist, burying her face against his chest. "I want your baby, I do. It's just…Hello! Zombie apocalypse. Cranky humans. The Unseen making me nuts. It's all a little scary."

"You're not alone, Kimber." He put his hands on her shoulders and pushed her gently back so he could look into her face. "If given a choice, would I want you to be vulnerable with child at this place and time? Absolutely not. Am I thrilled you're going to have my baby? Definitely." He brushed his lips over hers. "We'll handle this together."

She nodded and pulled away from him to walk back to the windows. She looked down, though he wasn't sure she saw anything. "I'm sorry I didn't tell you sooner. I was trying to get used to the idea."

"How long have you known?"

"Since we went out for tampons." Her voice was quiet and had a thread of guilt through it.

"Ah." He was surprised he wasn't angry at her for her deception. Maybe it would come later. "Not a trip for tampons, I take it."

She shook her head. "Pregnancy test. I peed on three test sticks just to be sure."

"And?"

"Two blue lines every time." She looked at him over her shoulder. He was happy to see a sparkle had lit her eyes. "I figure I'm about two months, give or take. It's been that long since I've had a period." She lifted one shoulder. "I thought it was stress making me late." She turned back toward the window. "You know— Oh my God!"

"What?" Duncan ran over to the window. The outer gates were open and a couple dozen zombies were already on the grounds, being fought off by the guards manning the gates. His first thought was to protect his lover and their baby. "Go to our rooms and stay there," he told Kimber. "I'll come get you when it's all over."

She scowled. "I don't think so. You need as many fighters out there as possible."

"Kimber—"

"Don't!" She slashed one hand through the air. "Do not start treating me like I'm some helpless, worthless weakling. I will fight to protect my home, Duncan. Don't try to stop me."

He vacillated for a few seconds, then, realizing she was right, gave in. "Grab your hatchet and any other fighters you can muster."

She nodded and sprinted toward the door. As she flung it open, she said, "We could use some of these alive."

"If we can," he said as he grabbed his tire iron from the credenza behind his desk. He headed down the stairs and hit the lobby the same time that Natalie did, coming up from the basement.

"It was Big Tom and his fricking idiot brotherhood," she snarled. She gripped her short sword in one hand. "They were trying to get out and didn't check to make sure it was clear before they opened the gates. Idiots."

Aodhán and Brigid came through the stairwell door, followed by Kimber, Leon, and several others. Since he didn't see Atticus, Duncan had to assume the big Roman was already outside in the midst of battle.

Duncan went outside, followed by the others, and waded into the fray. As he shoved his tire iron through the skull of a zombie, he looked toward the gates. "Get those damned things closed!" he yelled at the guards. He saw Atticus and Leon working their way toward the gates and knew as soon as they got there they'd get them closed. He turned his attention back to the fight. Another jab, then another, and zombies fell to his right and left.

He heard Kimber's little grunt as she drove her hatchet between the eyes of another shuffler. He found himself praying to whatever deity would listen that she'd be all right. It was his offspring—a miracle—inside her, and he didn't want to lose either one of them.

To his right, Natalie shoved the tip of her short sword through the skull of a shuffler. Pulling it free, she headed toward another one. But as she reached it, a zombie on the ground, toppled but not killed, grasped her ankle, throwing her off balance.

She shrieked and flung out a hand, trying to regain her equilibrium, and the zombie in front of her moved forward, arms out, hands grasping, intent on the potential feast it saw before it.

She fell to her hands and knees, kicking at the dead thing still clinging to her ankle while she rolled to her back and thrust her sword at the shuffler reaching for her from above.

"Natalie!" Aodhán roared her name and swung his sword, lopping off heads, sometimes three at a time, in his desperation to reach her. Duncan tried to get to her, too, all the while keeping an eye on Kimber. Aodhán gave another enraged yell and plunged his sword through the back of the zombie's skull. Thrusting the body aside, he pulled Natalie to her feet and into the shelter of his free arm.

Duncan glanced toward the gates and saw them closing. As Atticus latched them, screams went up from the other side of the fence.

"Oh my God." Kimber stood beside him. "There are people out there." She went over to Natalie and pulled her into a tight hug. "Are you all right?"

Natalie swiped one hand across her face, leaving a streak of blood on her cheek. "I'm okay. It didn't bite me."

"Thank the gods." Aodhán curled his free hand over Natalie's shoulder as if he couldn't bear to not have physical contact with her.

"You're sure you're okay?" Kimber released her, smiling faintly when Natalie fit herself against Aodhán's side once more.

Natalie nodded and leaned into Aodhán. He bent his head and pressed a kiss against her hair, though his eyes remained alert and constantly searching their surroundings.

Kimber glanced around, too, and saw that the vampires seemed to have things well in hand. Only a dozen or so zombies continued to stand, and even as she watched more fell.

After a few moments Natalie straightened and turned a glare on the few remaining shufflers. "We've got this. You go do what you can there," she said with a gesture toward the fence.

Duncan tipped his chin in acknowledgment. Leaving his army to take care of the cleanup, Duncan took Kimber's hand and together they ran to the gates. The guards stood a short distance behind them, protecting them from attack, though already the rest of the zombies were being taken care of. Duncan glanced at Atticus. "We need some of them alive," he said.

"Done." Atticus ran back toward the zombies, shouting for someone to bring him chains.

Duncan put his focus back on what was going on before him. Several zombies had dragged a man to the ground and were hunched over him, clearly feeding. A short distance away, the body of another man had also been turned into a banquet, but the torn-out throat indicated to Duncan that the human was already dead before they began eating. At least they wouldn't have to worry about reanimation.

The man closer to them screamed again, a high, shrill wail that choked off abruptly. "It's Big Tom," Duncan said. Before anyone could react, a guard closest to the fence shook his head. "It's too late. There's nothing we can do," Duncan added.

Poor bastard. He couldn't even imagine what it felt like to be eaten alive. To be *aware* that you were being eaten alive.

"I know." Kimber leaned against him, fighting for breath. As she watched the big man die, tears tracked down her cheeks.

Her soft heart was just one of the reasons he loved her. Duncan slid his arm around her waist and pulled her closer. She carried his child. *His child*. Their conversation had been interrupted, but they'd get back to it. They'd figure things out, like they always had.

Kimber turned her face into his shoulder. "As much of a pain in the butt as he was, I wouldn't have wished that on him, ever."

"Me neither." Duncan turned her away from the carnage. Together they stared at the dozen zombies chained in a group in the middle of the makeshift courtyard. "So, dear, I got you these zombies," he said. "Now what?"

Chapter Eleven

At dawn the next morning, Kimber stared at the zombies chained in the middle of the courtyard. Three of them were restrained thoroughly, chained side by side to three posts the vampires had driven into the ground after the fight. The zombies could barely twitch a finger let alone grab hold of someone. The others, eight of them, were held in a tight grouping in a hastily erected corral of sorts constructed with a chain-link fence and barbed wire.

It fascinated her to see the zombies press forward, impaling their skin on the barbed wire without flinching. They appeared to feel no pain, and she knew for a fact they felt no fear. Just overwhelming, unrelenting hunger. For human flesh.

She glanced at Maggie and Jason, standing beside her. They wore identical expressions of skepticism and apprehension mixed with a more than healthy dose of fright approaching panicked terror. Brigid, just behind them, so close her breasts brushed against the back of their arms, epitomized grace and unflappable serenity. The fey woman wore her confidence like a cloak.

Kimber envied her that ability. She'd had it, too, once upon a time. Back before she started the end of the world.

She glanced over at the entrance to the enclave building and saw Duncan and Atticus standing at the windows, looking out at them. He hadn't been thrilled with the idea of her conducting this experiment during daylight hours when the vamps couldn't be there to protect them, but she needed to be able to gauge the response the zombies had to the necromancers' supernatural attack. Doing this at night with flickering fire to light the area could have cost her valuable intel. She knew if anything went wrong, they'd both be out here to help, uncaring of the risk to themselves by being in the sunlight. She'd just have to make sure nothing went wrong.

She glanced to her left and saw Natalie, poised with pen and paper, ready to note her observations. To her right were about twenty humans, all armed with swords, fire pokers, tire irons...you name it. If it could be used to kill zombies, someone was going to use it. They were on standby in case any of the chains failed. It was overkill in her opinion, but Duncan had been adamant. Since she'd gotten fairly good about picking and choosing her battles—and she and Duncan still had to talk about her pregnancy—she'd let him have his way this time.

Kimber looked at the three immobilized zombies. "It's time," she said quietly. "Are you ready?"

Her human companions nodded, though their expressions

disagreed with their actions. When Kimber glanced at Brigid, the fey woman's placid expression never wavered. "Let us begin," she said.

"All right, people," Kimber said loudly enough for everyone to hear her. "We're going to make our way around behind those three." She pointed to the zombies trussed up like failed Houdinis. "So in a minute we'll need a distraction to keep their attention off of us." She looked at Maggie and Jason. "You're clear on what we're going to do? We'll crouch behind them and touch their ankles with one hand, and with our free hand we'll touch the necromancer closest to us."

"The person in the middle needs another hand," Maggie said. She rubbed one palm over her distended abdomen.

"Unnecessary." Brigid's cool voice held unwavering assurance. "I will act as a conduit between you three as well as between each of you and the Unseen."

Jason stared at her over his shoulder for a moment, then looked at Maggie. "I think you should sit this one out, honey," he said. He placed his hand over hers where it rested against her belly. "It's too dangerous. Kimber and I can do this." He glanced at Kimber with a grimace. "Probably."

Kimber wanted to tell Maggie to sit it out, too, but refrained. She knew how she'd feel if someone tried to take away her choices just because she was pregnant. While hormones might affect her emotions, they sure as hell didn't affect her decision-making ability. Jason made her uneasy. She wasn't sure how strong his abilities were or his tolerance to pain. Maggie, on the other hand, seemed much braver and most likely better able to soldier on through discomfort. She might need Maggie if Jason bailed.

"It's up to you," she told the other woman, even though she knew if Maggie lost this baby because of what they did here today, Kimber would never forgive herself. She tried not to think too closely about the fact that *she* could lose her baby just as easily.

"I can't just sit here and do nothing, especially when I have the ability to make a difference." Maggie squared her shoulders. "So let's do this thing."

And there it was. Like Maggie, Kimber couldn't sit on her thumbs and not try to fix what was so horribly wrong, even at the risk of her own life or that of her unborn child's.

Natalie and a few of the protectors started moving and making noise, drawing the attention of all the zombies, who immediately began to growl and snarl, jerking in their chains. Kimber, Maggie, Jason, and Brigid made their way behind the three. At one point their movements caused one of the zombies to jerk and stare at them until Natalie drew his attention away by getting close and yelling at him.

With his focus back on Natalie, Kimber and the others got into place. She and the two necromancers went to their knees behind the restrained zombies while Brigid moved forward to stand behind Kimber, who was in the middle. Kimber looked at Maggie and received a nod. Her glance at Jason gave her the same affirmation. They were ready.

Well, as ready as they'd ever be.

She took a deep breath and leaned forward to wrap her fingers around the ankle of the zombie in front of her. He started at the touch but continued to jerk in his restraints, trying to reach the tasty humans in front of him. Thankfully the chains held firm.

Jason and Maggie each took hold of a zombie ankle, and Brigid lightly grasped Kimber's shoulders. Kimber clasped Maggie's fingers with her left hand and felt Jason grip her upper arm on her right side.

"Here we go," Kimber whispered. "Focus now. Tap into the Unseen like you would have before, only now you're going to use it to force what's in the zombies back into the main body of the Unseen. Just remember, it feels different than it used to."

The fine hairs on the back of her neck lifted as the magic of the Unseen rippled. That feeling of darkness, of evil, that she now associated with the misty essence of the netherworld surged over her, trapping her breath in her throat for a moment. Her heart pounded; her palms grew clammy and cold. But she held on and continued to draw upon the Unseen.

As the power intensified, her gut cramped. She went hot, then cold. As more and more of the Unseen flowed into her, sweat broke out all over her body and her muscles began to tremble. "Now!" she cried. With a snarl she drew upon the malignant power surging from the Unseen and threw it out at the zombies. Floating spots of light sparkled across her field of vision, those dancing lights that meant her blood pressure was dangerously high. She kept pushing the power outward.

Her heartbeat thundered in her ears. Pain stabbed in her head. Still she pushed. Her heart stuttered, then doggedly beat on. From a distance she heard someone call out her name, heard the gasping cries of Jason and Maggie. And still. She. Pushed.

Her pulse pounded behind her eyes, making the early morning sunshine too bright, too piercing. She closed her eyes against the glare. With only instinct to guide her, she kept pushing the Unseen toward the zombies. Much like the stretching of a rubber band, she sensed when it was almost to the point of snapping. "Now pull the Unseen from the zombies and push it all back to its origin," she told the others. The misty energy of the netherworld seemed to lack the strength it needed to do what she wanted, almost as if the longer the apocalypse went on, the weaker its link to its origin. She couldn't think about what that meant right now; she couldn't lose her focus on the task at hand.

As she followed her own instructions, a slight bubble of warmth centered in her belly, stoking her flagging energy.

"It's working!" she heard Natalie yell.

Like the strings of a marionette being suddenly cut, the zombie she touched stopped all movement. She glanced up, squinting against the pain, and saw the male was completely limp, hanging in his chains. The other two were just as floppy. She looked toward the enclosure and saw all of the zombies there were on the ground, not moving.

"Check!" she ordered without moving her hand away from the ankle she held. "Don't let go yet," she told her compatriots.

Finally Natalie walked over and stood beside Maggie. "Stick a fork in 'em, Kimber. They're done."

A cheer went up.

They'd done it. She released her hold on the zombie and flexed her stiff fingers. Her entire body began to ache, and her head felt like it was going to explode. She winced with pain as she got to her feet. She helped Maggie up. "How're you doing?" she asked the pregnant woman. "How's the baby?"

"Fine. I think we're both fine." She glanced over at Jason. "Honey? How— Jason!"

Kimber turned just in time to see Jason's eyes flutter back in his skull and his body start to jerk. She grabbed his elbow as he went down and managed to keep him from hitting the ground hard.

His muscles contracted and flexed, making him flop like a landed fish, his lashes fluttering and his mouth open. Kimber didn't know what to do for him other than try to keep him from hurting himself, so she rolled him to his side and tried to brace him as best she could until the tremors finally passed. They seemed to go on forever but in reality probably lasted less than a minute. She blew out a sigh.

"Jason?" Maggie's voice quavered. She patted his cheek, her little fingers leaving small indentations on his skin. "Jason?"

Drawing in a shaky breath, Kimber reached down and placed her fingers against his carotid artery. Nothing. Oh. My. God. "Natalie!" she yelled. "Do we have a doctor?"

"Not yet." She knelt down next to Kimber. "What do you need?"

Kimber felt along Jason's chest until she reached his sternum. She centered her body over her hands, placed her palms down, fingers laced together, and started compressions. "Make sure his airway is clear," she instructed.

While Kimber pressed his chest up and down, Natalie counted to thirty.

"Anything?" Kimber asked.

Natalie put her fingers to his throat, then placed her hand in front of his mouth. "Nothing."

Kimber started chest compressions again, with Natalie counting and checking his breathing. They did this for several minutes, Kimber's arms and back beginning to feel the strain, until Maggie finally cried out, "Enough!" She sobbed and knelt next to Jason. "That's enough," she said more quietly. "He's gone." She brushed his hair away from his forehead. "He's gone."

They gave her a few minutes; then Natalie cupped Maggie's elbows and helped her to her feet. "Come on, hon," she urged the grief-stricken woman. "Let's get you inside."

Kimber struggled to her feet, nearly overcome with fatigue. Seeing Natalie's legal tablet on the ground, she bent and picked it up, then stumbled as a wave of dizziness assailed her upon standing.

Only Natalie's quick reflexes kept her from pitching forward onto her face. "Let's get you inside as well," she said. "You need to rest." She glanced at Maggie and Brigid, her expression one of compassion. "You all need to."

Kimber started toward the entrance, knowing the men in the courtyard would get the zombie bodies to the other side of the fence. They were safe once more, but for how long?

* * *

Duncan took Kimber into his arms as soon as she came into the building. He'd hated letting her be outside without him there to protect her, but once the sun had turned him into a burned-out husk, he wouldn't have been of much use. "Are you all right?" He swept his hand over her hair and cupped the back of her head.

She wrapped her arms around his waist and snuggled in. Her head moved in the affirmative against his chest. "But Jason…"

Her tremulous sigh hurt his heart. Damn it. He wanted to wrap her up and protect her from everything. "I'm sorry, sweetheart." Keeping one arm around her waist, he turned and guided her toward the stairs. "Let's get you into bed. You look exhausted."

"I am." They started up in silence. After three flights, she lifted the legal pad and showed it to him. "But we did it, Duncan." Her excitement came through in spite of her fatigue.

"I saw." He didn't want to douse her ebullience, but it was going to take forever to stop the apocalypse if they could only do it to a dozen zombies at a time, especially if it cost them a necromancer. "What went wrong with Jason?" he asked.

"I don't know." She started to say more but then gasped as her legs gave beneath her.

"Let's get you upstairs." Duncan swept her into his arms and carried her up the remaining stairs and all the way into their bedroom, where he lay her down on the bed. He took the tablet from her hand and placed it on the nightstand. "We'll look at that once you've gotten some sleep."

Just as he started to pull a light blanket over her, she opened her eyes and shook her head, struggling to sit up. "I need to take a shower." She held her right hand out. "I touched a dead guy." Her forehead scrunched. "Ooh, and then I touched you. You need a shower, too."

He grinned. "Works for me." Stroking her cheek, he watched one emotion after another rush across her face. Mischief followed by sadness as she no doubt recalled the recent death of a new friend. "Come on," he whispered. "Let's take that shower."

He lifted her into his arms and carried her into the bathroom, where he gently drew off her clothes. After he made sure she could remain standing on her own, though she swayed with exhaustion, he quickly stripped and turned on the shower. Waiting until the water heated up, he urged her into the stall and followed behind, closing the frosted glass door behind him.

Duncan used her vanilla-scented body wash to tenderly cleanse her, starting with her slender fingers, and did his best to keep her hair dry. As he worked his way over her slender body, he took care with her breasts and the folds of her sex, not wanting to overstimulate her. As much as he wanted her—he always wanted her—right now she needed sleep.

He rinsed her thoroughly and turned off the water. He slid open the door and grabbed a large bath towel, blotting the water off her skin. He followed up with lotion as quickly as he could, then picked her up and carried her back to the bed where he placed her on the mattress and slid the sheet up over her naked, sleepy form.

Her eyes were closed, lashes casting shadows on her pale cheeks. She had one hand on her still-taut abdomen. He sat beside her and rested his hand over hers. "Is the baby all right?"

Her eyes fluttered open for a second but closed right away as if it was too much effort to keep them open. "I think so," she said, her voice a little slurred. "I don't feel any different." And then just like that she was out.

Duncan moved to a bedside chair and watched her sleep, keeping an eye on her respiration, so glad to see her breasts rising and falling evenly. He should check on the others, but he knew if anyone else was having issues, someone would let him know. Right now his place was with Kimber.

He raked his hand through his hair. When he'd seen Jason go down, Duncan had almost raced outside to get to Kimber, to make sure he was there in case she had a similar reaction. Only Atticus and Leon holding him back had kept him in the building. While she hadn't gone into convulsions and died like Jason had, he'd seen the toll fighting zombies in this way took. He'd seen the paleness of her skin, the labored breathing, the rise in her blood pressure.

It could have just as easily been her, and their unborn child. He had to make a decision, and the one his gut was leaning toward would make Kimber a very unhappy little necromancer. But he couldn't allow her to continue putting herself at such risk, even if she seemed to spring back after such exhaustion without any problems. He'd never been an almost-dad before, and he knew he was going to botch things up, but he couldn't help himself. He needed to keep his family safe.

While Kimber slept, Duncan was given periodic reports on what was going on. The zombies were cleared out of the courtyard. The remaining necromancer, Maggie, was resting and seemed to be fine, her baby, too. Brigid was also in her room, recuperating from her efforts.

Two hours later, Kimber's legs shifted on the mattress, then she stretched and yawned. As her eyes opened, Duncan leaned forward in the chair he'd placed next to the bed. "Sleep well?"

She frowned. "Why didn't you climb in with me?"

"I didn't want to disturb you."

She turned onto her side to face him, curling one arm beneath the pillow. "You wouldn't have." Her gaze went to the tablet on the nightstand. "Did you look at Nat's notes?"

He glanced at it. "Hmm. I didn't see where there was anything particularly enlightening, but you might think differently." He reached out and grabbed the glass of water he'd placed there while she was sleeping. Making an upward motion with his other hand, he said, "Come on. Up you go. You need to hydrate."

She scooted up to lean her back against the headboard. She took the water from him and downed it in one go, letting out a loud, satisfied sigh when she finished.

Duncan took the glass from her and set it aside. "You feel good about what happened? I mean, except for Jason."

She pondered that a moment, then nodded. "We did it, right?"

"Yes, though on a very small number."

"At first I didn't think it was working. It was almost like the Unseen in the zombies wasn't strong enough, was somehow too diluted to do what we needed it to do." She nibbled on her bottom lip. "I had the thought, during all that, that the longer the apocalypse goes on, the weaker the link becomes between the main body of the Unseen and the bits that are in the zombies." She stared at him. "Duncan, if that's the case, then we're running out of time. We won't be able to push the Unseen that's animating the zombies out of them and back into itself. We'll be trapped here for the rest of our lives, keeping the zombies at bay. And how long will that last? Eventually, we'll run out of food and a safe place to live." She rested her hand on her abdomen. "I don't want to raise my child in a zombie-infested world."

He pondered that and knew the decision he'd already reached had been the right one. Knowing this was going to make her angry, he added, "Listen, I don't want you to try again. This killed one necromancer, and we don't know why, and both you and Maggie were drained. I know this isn't what you want to hear, but if you won't stop this for yourself, think about the baby."

Instead of flaring up at him, she sighed and closed her eyes. "I think the baby gave me a little boost in energy," she said.

"What!"

She looked at him. "Right before the zombies dropped, I felt…" She placed her palms on her abdomen and pressed down. "There was this surge of warmth here, and then I heard Nat say it was working."

Fear clutched at his insides. "You drew energy from our baby? Like you did with Atticus?"

"No, of course not." Her eyes widened and one hand came up to cover her mouth. Tears sparkled in her eyes. She dropped her hand to her lap, defeat and despair drawing lines on her face. "Oh my God. Not on purpose, Duncan. You have to believe me. I didn't consciously think about doing it."

He got up and perched on the edge of the bed and took her hands in his. "I know you didn't, sweetheart. But what remains is that it happened. The baby needs all its energy to grow, to survive." He brought her hands to his mouth and pressed kisses on her knuckles. "Something else is bothering you. What is it?"

She leaned her head against the headboard. "If it's getting harder to get the Unseen out of zombies, what about the bit that's in me?" Her fingers tightened around his. "Duncan, I'm really scared about having this inside me."

"Do you think Brigid and Maggie might be able to help you?"

"I don't know." Her eyes widened. "Wait. Maggie! Is she all right? What about her baby?"

"They're both fine," he soothed. They sat there for several moments; then he said, "Do you want something to eat? You're probably starving."

"I could eat, yeah." He helped her off the bed, holding her as she stumbled. "Wow, that really took it out of me, I guess. I still feel a little fuzzy."

He slipped his arm around her waist. "Come on. Let's go out to the living room and I'll have the kitchen prepare you something."

They walked out to the main living area and he settled her on the sofa. Just as he was about to straighten, she reached up and grabbed his hand. "Duncan, thank you," she whispered.

"For what?" he asked. All of a sudden he couldn't move; his throat worked to say something but he seemed powerless to do so. Her hand, where it curled around his, grew hot. He staggered, feeling like his legs were going to give out, and tried to jerk away from her. He couldn't. After what seemed like an eternity, she gasped and let go of him so abruptly he teetered, then fell on his ass.

"Oh my God! Duncan, I didn't mean it." She sat forward on the couch, her face pale, her eyes pleading with him.

His head felt like it was going to explode. All of his nerve endings flared, sending pain like he'd never felt throughout his body. "You…" He shook his head. "What the hell?"

Had this been what she'd done to Atticus? No wonder he'd been so pissed off. Duncan wasn't too happy about it, either. But he did notice Kimber looked much more alert, and his pain was fading.

"I am so sorry." Her hands fluttered as if she wanted to reach out for him but knew she couldn't. Shouldn't. "I'm so, so sorry." She curled her fingers into fists. "It's this Unseen that's inside me. It wanted your power, your *life*. We have to get it out of me, Duncan. Before I kill someone."

Chapter Twelve

Duncan watched Kimber push food around on her plate. It had been three days since she'd inadvertently siphoned energy from him, and he didn't think she'd eaten more than a few bites since. She'd done what she was doing now—sighing and looking dejected. Defeated.

It was a look he hated to see on his strong, indomitable woman. It was one he planned on getting rid of, if he could figure out how.

They sat on the sofa in their living room. He had been pretending to read a mystery novel while she pretended to eat. Now he reached over and put his hand on hers, stilling her movement. She jerked her hand away and fisted it in her lap.

He hated this. They were right back where they'd been after she'd drained Atticus, except now he was the one reaching out only to have her flinch away.

"Sweetheart, you need to eat," he urged. "You've hardly had anything in the last couple of days."

She looked at him, remorse and trepidation dark in her eyes. "I know. I just…" She sighed. "I can't forget the look on your face, Duncan. You were so shocked and in so much pain. I did that to you. Me." She looked down at her hands in her lap. "I don't know how you can stand to even be in the same room as me."

"It's not you. It's the Unseen." He leaned over and put his hand on hers again, tightening his fingers when she tried to draw away. "Don't," he said. "Don't pull away from me. We're in this together, Kimber. You and me, we'll figure this out." When she nodded and stopped yanking her arm, he stroked his thumb over the back of her hand. "Now, please, eat something."

She drew in a breath and held it a moment, then released it. This time when she tugged at her hand he let it go, and she picked up her fork again. Several minutes later her plate was nearly clean. "That's it," she said, dropping the fork on the plate. She leaned back against the sofa. "I'm full."

Without a word, Duncan picked up the plate and carried it into the kitchen, then came back and took his seat on the couch again. He took her hands in his and stared into her eyes. "I've read through Natalie's notes again, and remembering how things went the other day, I think the solution to stopping the apocalypse isn't by using zombies. It's by using vampires. Namely me."

"No!" Kimber jerked her hands away and jumped to her feet. "Duncan, you know what happened when I latched on to you by accident. If I did it on purpose, I could kill you." She dashed tears off her cheeks. "No. I won't use you that way."

"Kimber—"

"No." She walked away from him to stand in front of the fire-place. With her back to him, she said, "You don't understand how it made me feel. How tempting it was to…" She broke off with a muttered imprecation.

"How tempting what was?" he prompted.

She whirled around. "To keep all that power for myself. To use it to lash out for my own purposes. Not to fight zombies. To take revenge on people who cross me." She wrapped her arms around her waist. "It scared me, Duncan, that desire. Because I knew I could never have enough."

"Do you think you would feel this way without the Unseen in you?"

She shrugged. Tears glittered in her eyes but she stubbornly refused to let them fall. "I don't have anything to base a con-clusion on, Duncan. This is all so new. I've never drawn energy from a vampire until I did it with Atticus. I didn't know I could. Maybe I couldn't before. Maybe it took having a bit of the Unseen inside for me to have that ability." She paused and chewed on her bottom lip. "What if…" She drew in a breath. Eyes wide, she asked, "What if it's a piece of Eduardo?"

"What?"

"Just listen to me for a minute." She licked her lips and started walking back and forth in front of the fireplace, her hands flapping in front of her as she paced. "Maggie told me that when I was reanimating Richard Whitcomb, you know, the Lazarus that started this whole thing?" At his nod, she con-tinued. "At the very same time across town, Maddalene had another necromancer trying to raise Eduardo. I guess she got tired of waiting on me."

He frowned. "I'm not connecting the dots. It's not the first time more than one necromancer did their job at the same time. Why would it make a difference then?"

She halted and looked at him. "Because she decided that adding the necromancer's blood to the ritual would strengthen the bond and ensure Eduardo's resurrection, so she killed the necromancer. She was wrong." She picked up her pacing again. "But Eduardo's spirit was already on its way and it needed someplace to go. He needed someplace to go, and he didn't want to go back to the Unseen. So he went where the power was the strongest."

"He went to you." Duncan had always had a sense of pride in Kimber's abilities. It had pleased him to know she was the strongest necromancer in the area, perhaps even the state.

She nodded. "He went to me," she agreed. "That would be why it got so weird, the way Whitcomb looked, like something evil was inside him. And toward the end, the way he talked to me, even then I thought someone else—or some*thing* else—was speaking through him."

He pondered that for a few minutes. "Yeah, Eduardo was a sick son of a bitch. Maddalene was the only one sorry to see him destroyed."

"I need to go talk to Natalie."

He raised his brows.

"She was my assistant. Even if she wasn't with me that night, she went with me on plenty of raisings. She has insight." She started toward the door. "I need to talk to her."

"I'll come with you."

"Duncan…" She placed her hands on his chest. "I don't even know what I'm going to ask her. She's my sounding board, that's all. I promise I'm not going to come up with a plan and run off half-cocked."

"You go running off anywhere, you'd better come get me first," he told her.

"Yeah, 'cause then I can run off whole-cocked." Her grin was fleeting, as was the kiss she placed at the corner of his mouth. "I love you." Then she was out the door.

Duncan scrubbed the back of his neck. They couldn't continue on the way they were, living behind fortified walls while the zombies kept on coming. Their supplies were dwindling and would eventually be too small to sustain them. Kimber was right. They had to end the apocalypse.

She was the expert on this. He had to trust her. He didn't have to like it.

* * *

Natalie finished taking off her clothes and stepped up to an equally naked Aodhán. She rubbed her hands across his strong collarbone, then trailed her fingers through the dark hair that lightly dusted his pectorals. Lower down, his cock stood long and proud from its nest of dark hair. She gave him a little push toward the bed. "Why don't you sit down and let me return the favor you did for me a while ago?"

He grinned and sat. His thighs were rock hard. He positioned his hands behind him and leaned back slightly, muscles flexing in his arms as they bore his weight. "I know better than to get in the way of a woman on a mission, and you have that look."

"You better believe it." She wanted to taste him, to pleasure him. Then once he got his second wind, she wanted to fuck him like a hyper bunny rabbit. With a smile, she wrapped her hand around his cock.

He was silken skin wrapped around steel. So thick. So hot. Settling her forearms on either side of his muscular thighs, she worked on slowly sending him into orbit. He felt so good against her tongue. As she made love to his cock with her mouth, he sat forward. His roughened hands roamed over her shoulders, her back, then into her hair, gripping her head to direct her movements.

"Great gods, do you have any idea how sexy you are, on your knees with those pretty breasts swaying and your lips around my cock?" When she took him to the back of her throat and swallowed, he groaned. "Fuck. Do that again."

She did, loving the sound of his sensual tension building higher and higher. With one hand she reached between his legs and stroked his balls. His hands tightened in her hair. The sac of flesh in her palm drew up closer to his body. He shouted, his cock jerking in her mouth, and his release streamed into her throat in hot, heavy jets. He thrust against her with a final panting growl, and she swallowed one last time. As he pulled away, she gave the tip of his cock another loving lick. She could do this for him every day and never get tired of it. To show him that his pleasure mattered to her, pleased her in a primal way. She guessed it set something off in her inner cavewoman.

He let go of her hair and stroked his fingers against her scalp where his hands had been fisted tightly. Then he bent and wrapped his hands around her upper arms, lifting her up to rest on top of him as he lay back on the bed. "That was amazing. Thank you, *mo chroí*." He rubbed his hands up and down her bare back. With a slight growl, he rolled over, caging her beneath him. He pressed his groin against hers. "Give me a few minutes, and we'll find out if your pussy is as tight around my cock as I think it's going to be."

"You're such a sweet talker, Aodhán. I don't know why you're still single." She tried to keep a straight face, but at his put-on look, his over-the-top wounded expression, she laughed. Bending her knees, she cradled him against her pelvis. "But I'm glad you are. That means you're available to me."

"Only to you, Natalie. Always." He brought his head down to hers and gave her such a sweet, slow kiss it brought tears to her eyes.

She cupped his dear face in her hands and returned the caress. As their tongues twined together, she wrapped her legs around his hips and pulled him closer, her heels pressing against the backs of his thighs. She felt a twitch of interest from his cock, but before she could do much about it, she heard knocking at the front door.

He reared up, frowning down at her when she showed no indication of moving. "Aren't you going to see who that is?" he asked.

"Nope." She trailed her fingers across his shoulders, squeezing here and there, testing the firmness of those bulging muscles. He was so big and brawny, and she knew his strength would only be used to protect her, never to harm her. The knowledge filled her with delight.

"It might be important," he said. She could tell by the look in his eyes his attention was beginning to focus on her once more and he wasn't overly concerned about who might be at the door.

"*This* is important," she responded. She started to draw him down to her. The person at the door knocked again, louder this time, and it sounded like whoever it was also gave the door a few kicks. Natalie sighed and closed her eyes. "It's Kimber."

"I figured. She's the only one I know who's that impatient." After pressing a kiss to her forehead, Aodhán rolled off her and got to his feet in a single, fluid movement that made her gasp. God, he was so beautiful it hurt to look at him sometimes. "You'd better get dressed and answer the door before she has someone let her in."

The pounding came again. "Oh, for crying out loud." Natalie got up and pulled on a blouse and jeans, buttoning the shirt as she stalked through the living room. "This had better be good." She yanked open the door.

"Hello to you, too," Kimber responded with a frown. When Aodhán came out of the bedroom, tucking his shirt into his leather pants, her mouth formed an O of surprise before tilting into a broad smile. "Well, well, well. It's about dayum time, people."

"Oh, shut up." Natalie tried unsuccessfully to fight back a blush. "What do you want?"

Kimber didn't say anything right away, just looked from Natalie to Aodhán and back again. Then her eyes went big and round. "Oh my God. I interrupted you right in the middle of…I'm the definition of *coitus interruptus*. I'm so sorry. Look, I'll just go and you two can get back to…things. Things that I don't want to hear about, because, you know, TMI and all that."

"Kimber, stop." Natalie knew her friend sometimes rambled on when she got embarrassed, and this was clearly one of those times. She wasn't sure which one of them was redder in the face.

"It's all right, *mo chara*." Aodhán stopped beside Kimber and curved his hand over her shoulder. "You didn't interrupt anything that Natalie and I can't get back to with equally satisfying results."

Kimber's eyes closed and she let out a small groan. "Okay, fine. Just shut up about it already."

Natalie laughed. When Aodhán bent and placed a gentle and too-brief kiss against her mouth, she sighed and leaned against him for a moment.

"I'm going to check in with Brigid, see how she's feeling," he said. "I'll be back later, all right?"

"You'd better be." She watched him go through the door, then turned her attention on her friend. "Okay, what's up? And it had better be good, because we were just about to, you know."

Kimber grimaced. "I know. Sorry. My timing sucks."

Natalie went into the living room. "So, what's so important you practically beat down my door?" she asked as she sat down on the couch.

Kimber plopped down beside her with a long, loud sigh.

"Duncan thinks it would be better for necromancers to use vamps instead of zombies to push the Unseen back."

"Really?" Natalie frowned. "That's quite a turnaround."

"Tell me about it." Kimber's laugh held more than a dollop of misery. "But I don't think he'll let me test the theory unless I agree to use him. And that's not gonna happen, no matter what the king of the vampires says."

Oh, boy. Natalie knew her friend had always kicked against authority, especially those who tried to keep her from doing something she believed she should. "And?"

Kimber gave a snort. "He really can't stop me."

Natalie pursed her lips. "Ah, but yes he could. He could lock you in your quarters, post more guards, any number of things. You know the only way this is going to happen is if he lets you." She tilted her head to one side. "But am I missing something? I know he'd like to stop the apocalypse, and you just told me he said you could use him, so why wouldn't he let you?"

Red streaked across Kimber's cheeks. "Oh, right. I haven't told you yet." Her gaze met Natalie's. "I'm pregnant," Kimber said.

"What!" Natalie stared at her, her mouth open and eyes wide. "Oh my God! You're just full of surprises lately. First about being able to draw energy from vampires—Atticus *and* Duncan—and now this." She leaned over and hugged her friend. "I'm so happy for you." As she pulled back, she saw the look on Kimber's face and realized the other woman wasn't exactly overjoyed. "Wait. Maybe I shouldn't be happy for you?"

Kimber shook her head. "No, no. You can be happy for me.

I'm happy for me. Mostly. It's just…" She swiped at a tear. "I have some of the Unseen in me, and when I drained energy from Atticus and then again from Duncan, there was some part of me, some small, gleeful part that wanted more, that wanted to take all they had." Her hazel eyes took on a green cast as her emotions grew. "I could kill him."

"And it's possible you could *not*." Natalie covered Kimber's hand with hers. "You don't want to raise a child in this environment. What other choice do you have but to try to put down all zombies once and for all?"

"I could refuse to use him, make him let me use someone else."

"Who else? Atticus?" At the repulsed expression on Kimber's face, Natalie knew the idea of sacrificing anyone else was repugnant to her friend. But Natalie kept pushing. "Or maybe Leon?"

"Stop. I know what you're doing." Kimber scowled. "There was a difference in the level of power. It's…muted, for want of a better description, in the zombies. In vampires it's unfiltered. Much more potent. If I were to do this, do you think it would work?"

Natalie thought about it for a few minutes. While she wasn't a necromancer herself, she'd worked with Kimber for a few years and had observed her at work. She was good. The best, in Natalie's admittedly biased opinion. But thankfully it wasn't just her who thought that. Others had commented on Kimber's amazing ability as well. If anyone could do this, it was Kimberly Treat.

"If the difference in power is what you say it is," Natalie said slowly, "then, yes, I think you could do it. Especially if you use more necromancers and have Brigid act as your focus." She began to get excited at the prospect. "You could set up a domino effect, so that the power to push out the Unseen goes from zombie to zombie. You start with just a few and the effect cascades from there." She paused and tapped her chin. "I don't know if it would travel across the oceans, but we could at least take care of this continent."

"Continent." Kimber sighed. Closing her eyes, she leaned her head back against the sofa. "Would you listen to yourself? 'We could take care of a continent.' Do you have any idea how daunting that sounds?" She rolled her head back and forth. "Continent. Crap."

And there it was. This was so much bigger than their little corner of the world. It had always been, of course, but survival had necessitated focusing things homeward. But to truly make the situation better, they couldn't merely take care of themselves and call it quits. They had to look at the whole world, beginning with the Americas.

"I don't think I can use Duncan." Kimber's voice was reed-thin and the raw look of misery in her eyes was heart wrenching. "I love him too much. But I know he won't put any of his people in danger. Oh, God. What am I going to do?"

Natalie shivered. She didn't have an answer. She was a spectator in this; she had no special powers to offer. It would be up to Kimber and Duncan, and those like them, to make things right.

She only hoped they survived.

Chapter Thirteen

After talking things over with Natalie, Kimber went back to her suite, feeling torn. But at least she had the beginnings of a plan in place, and the more she thought about it the more excited she became. To start with just a few zombies and have the effects branch out from there would be like imploding a building upon itself. The apocalypse would pretty much take care of itself.

She needed to bounce this idea off Duncan, because if it worked the way she hoped it would, whoever she used to draw energy from would be put at risk for a very short period of time. Much shorter a time than when she'd used Atticus to put down that batch on the way back from the drug store. When she entered the suite, Duncan glanced up from where he was looking over some papers at the head of the dining room table.

"Work never stops, huh?" She went over and pulled out a chair to sit at the spot on his left.

"Unfortunately, no. I've sent a runner to Xavier Vachon asking him to send down a necromancer, if he has one, to replace Jason. Just in case we go through with this. I've also asked for any food he can spare." He shoved the documents away and scrubbed a big hand across his jaw. "We're clearing out some land to plant a good-sized garden, but quite honestly I think we're going to have to start rationing food before anything's ready to be harvested. I've told Atticus to hold off on bringing more humans here until our foodstuffs are restocked."

Kimber frowned. She didn't like the idea of barring admittance to anyone who needed shelter. "But if we know of humans out there, we can't just leave them. It's not safe."

"We can't feed them, Kimber. In another month we'll barely be able to feed the ones we already are housing here." He scowled. "This is what I get for allowing a human to keep track of inventory."

Anger started a slow boil inside her. "You know, you keep referring to us like we're stupid. Worse than stupid, even."

His scowl deepened. "What're you talking about?"

"Just now, when you said 'this is what I get for allowing a human to keep track of inventory,' and a couple of weeks ago you were equally condescending about me and my *little* friends wanting to play with zombies. Oh, and let's not forget your crack about 'you humans' wanting to go waltzing around in the park." Hurt rose to join the anger. She pointed a finger at him. "Be honest. You don't like us very much, do you? We're nothing more to you than a meal ticket. Literally."

He turned to face her more fully. "Kimber, you know that's not true."

"Isn't it?" She pushed to her feet so violently she knocked over the chair. It clattered to the floor and with a snarl she shoved it aside. The rage built, roiling through her like a boiling tide of red-hot magma. Even as she was aware of the anger and knew it was out of proportion to the conversation, she wanted to be even more furious, wanted to feed that hungry darkness inside her. "It's always 'you humans this' and 'you humans that.'"

He slowly stood. His face impassive, he said, "And you've never once spoken disparagingly about vampires?"

She snapped her mouth closed on a reply. She had, damn it. Some of the rage fizzled as if ice water had doused it. "That's not the point. Stop trying to distract me."

"Not trying to distract you, sweetheart. I'm just saying the spaghetti sauce shouldn't call the ketchup a son of a tomato."

Ooh, he was infuriating. How like a vampire to use an analogy with foods that were red. "So you respect us, then? Humans, I mean."

"I don't respect all humans, nor do I respect all vampires." He lifted one shoulder in a shrug. " His serious gaze held hers. "I respect you. I respect Natalie. And Maggie, I suppose, though I don't know her very well."

Yeah, right. He said that now, but in a few minutes she wouldn't be surprised if he started spouting off about humans again. He'd told her he loved her, but did he really? How could he? She was a danger to him. To his people, which he'd made very clear didn't include humans. Humans were necessary to vampires' survival, but they were clearly a nuisance to him, and she didn't see him making friends with any of them except for

Natalie. And he was only friends with her because of her relationship with Kimber. Kind of a twofer.

"It's not the species that dictates my respect. It's how a person uses their intelligence. You know that." He moved closer and wrapped his hands gently around her upper arms. "Kimber, tell me where the hell all of this is coming from."

Gah. She was going crazy. The Unseen inside her was making her insane. She pulled away from him. "Nowhere. It's nothing. Never mind." She walked into the living room and stood in front of the empty fireplace. "I think I have a plan to stop the apocalypse."

As he joined her in the living room, she heard a barely imperceptible sigh from him. Good grief, she was only two months pregnant, emotional, and hyped up because of the Unseen inside her, and he was already losing his patience with her. What would he be like when she was eight months pregnant, felt as huge as a house, ate everything in sight, and was even crankier than she was now?

"What's the plan?" he asked as he sat down on the sofa. Apparently he was going to let her earlier attitude—and really lame response to him calling her out on it—slide for now.

After she explained about her notion of a domino effect, his expression indicated his intrigue with the idea. "You really think it would work?"

"Yeah, I think it could work." She sat beside him on the couch. "We'd be using the Unseen that is in you, which is pure Unseen, untainted by Eduardo, to push the corrupt Unseen out of the zombies."

His brows furrowed. "But won't that corrupt the Unseen?"

She shook her head. "The Unseen itself is neither good nor bad. It just is. It's the netherworld where all life begins and where souls return after death. It's where Eduardo's essence was to begin with." She settled back into the corner of the sofa, sitting cross-legged to face Duncan on the other end.

He stared at her a few moments; then his shoulders slumped slightly as if he'd been holding himself in a rigid posture he just couldn't maintain any longer. "When do you want to do this?"

"We'll need a few days to prepare. This is assuming we get a third necromancer." She bit her lip. "I really don't think it'll work with just two. Especially since Maggie and I are both pregnant." When his mouth opened, she held up one hand. "Don't, Duncan. I'll do everything I can to not risk the baby, but I have to do this. And you know it."

His chin dipped. "Yes." His voice was low. Quiet. Sad. For the first time since she'd known him, his eyes glittered with tears. "I don't want to lose you, Kimber. Either one of you."

Her own eyes went a little misty. "I don't want to lose you, either. It's not just me and the baby that will be in danger, you know. I'll be drawing energy from you. You'll be the source of the Unseen to push out to all the zombies. What if I take it too far? Hold on too long?" The last word came out on a wail, and she brought her hands up to her face, bowing over as grief and fear assailed her. She wanted to stop the zombie apocalypse, but not with Duncan's life. That cost was too high.

But she didn't want to try to raise her baby while fighting for survival surrounded by a bunch of flesh eaters, either.

Duncan's arms came around her, and he lifted her to place her on his lap, pressing her head to his shoulder. She clasped her hands around his neck and held on through the storm of tears. Vaguely she heard him murmuring to her, words she couldn't discern over the sounds of her weeping and her pulse whooshing in her ears.

Her body shook, her sobs breaking loose in heaving waves, coming from somewhere very deep within her. For nine months she'd believed she'd been the cause of the Outbreak. Now she knew she wasn't. But it looked like she could end it, but at what cost?

Kimber turned her face into Duncan's neck and after a few minutes they began to abate and finally subsided. All the tension left her, leaving her limp in his arms. With his fingers beneath her chin, he tilted her face up to look down at her. She made eye contact with him but said nothing.

"We'll get through this, sweetheart," he said. "You have to believe that."

"I want to believe it." She sniffed, then smiled when he dug out a clean white handkerchief from his back pocket and handed it to her. She wiped her eyes and blew her nose. Crumpling the material in her fist, she whispered, "You're the only person I know who carries one of those around."

"One never knows when a lady in distress might need a hankie." He swiped his thumb over her cheek, scooping up a last bit of moisture. "I love you, Kimber." He dropped his mouth on hers, lips moving, seeking. When her lips parted, his tongue stroked inside, languid, tender, moving her to tears again, though she managed to stem the tide.

"Make love with me." She dropped the handkerchief onto the coffee table and fisted her hands in his shirt. "I need to feel you inside me."

He muttered a curse and in a deft movement swept her beneath him. He settled his hips against her pelvis, making space for himself in the cradle of her thighs.

She could feel the length of his erection pressing against her mound. With greedy hands she tugged his shirttail from his slacks. "Too many clothes."

He stood and stripped, his motions no less sexy for their efficiency. Before she could do much more than blink, he had her clothes off, too, and came back down on top of her. He kept his upper body off her but rolled his groin against her.

Kimber pushed her hips up and moaned at the feel of Duncan's hard length sliding against the lips of her sex. Just a couple of strokes against her labia and she was slick and hot. "Please," she moaned.

His mouth closed wetly around her nipple, suckling her with hard pulls of lips and tongue. He gave her other breast the same sweet treatment, acting like he could stay where he was for the next year or so.

She wasn't going to have any of that. "Inside me, Duncan," she demanded. "Stop fooling around and fuck me."

He lifted his head and stared down at her. One corner of his mouth quirked. "And here I thought women wanted foreplay. You seem to complain if you don't get it."

She smiled sweetly with bared teeth. "We want foreplay to get our motors revving. My motor's already at about eight

RPMs, so foreplay is just pissing me off." She grabbed his shoulders, her nails biting into his skin. "Get. Inside. Me. Now."

The other side of his mouth curled up. "Yes, ma'am." His big hands slid over her inner thighs and parted them slowly. He raised her left leg and hooked it over his right forearm and placed the head of his big, swollen cock at the slick entrance to her body. She trembled at the feel of his hot flesh against her, the intimacy of his touch. Leaning over her, he braced himself on his elbow and kissed her, murmuring against her lips, "You're so beautiful. I love you."

He pressed into her, the broad head sliding in slowly, his girth stretching her sheath. He continued his slow glide in until his balls rested against the curve of her behind. Sensual pleasure tightened the lean lines of his face, glittered with silver fire in his eyes. Then he pulled back until only the head of his cock was inside her. With a taut smile, he began to thrust, in and out, slow strokes that gradually picked up speed until his hips hammered her. The sounds of flesh slapping against flesh filled the room.

He tilted her pelvis and on each inward stroke he touched that sensitive bundle of nerves in her passage, making her tighten around him, causing her to gasp and moan with every jab of his hips. Lifting her head, she watched his possession of her, his cock coated with her juices, sliding into her pussy to the root.

Another adjustment on her position increased the friction on her clit. As her arousal heightened, her body went taut. Higher and higher he took her until her inner muscles clamped down, clenching and releasing in a shattering climax. She screamed, her fingers digging into his hips.

He thrust hard two more times and then shoved deep, holding himself still inside her and giving a shout of his own as he came. His hot ejaculate jetted into her sex. All she could do was hold on to him. His head tilted back, features relaxing in the aftermath, and he reversed their positions so he was on his back and she lay on top of him, their intimate connection unbroken.

Breathing hard, she rested her head on his chest and snuggled into him. That had been amazingly intense, and right now, she had no doubts whatsoever that he loved and wanted her.

"I didn't hurt you, did I?" His voice was raspy and deeply satisfied.

"Of course not." She rubbed her cheek against his chest. "You gave me exactly what I wanted."

His hands rubbed up and down her back, and they remained as they were for several minutes. She found herself wishing they could stay like this forever, just the two of them at peace with themselves and the world.

A knock at the door ended that little daydream.

She sighed and climbed off him, moaning softly when his semihard cock slid out of her. "Later, baby." She gave him a wink.

His mouth tilted in that half-smile she loved and in silence they hurriedly dressed. He made sure she was decent before he walked over to the door and pulled it open.

Kimber moved to a spot where she could see who was there. "Hi, Leon," she called out, and waggled her fingers at him.

"Hello, Ms. Treat," he responded. He looked at Duncan and said, "Xavier Vachon and a human named Hunter McKay are here. Vachon says McKay's a necromancer." He glanced over Duncan's shoulder to Kimber, then focused on Duncan again. "I put them across the hall in your office." By the expression on his face, he clearly wanted to know why there was yet another necromancer on the premises, but he was too well trained to ask.

"Thank you, Leon. We'll be right over. Would you please bring Maggie and Brigid up?"

Leon nodded and turned away.

Duncan closed the door and gathered up his shoes and socks. He sat on the sofa and pulled them on.

Kimber did the same.

"Are you ready for this?" He looped his arms around her and clasped his hands loosely behind her back.

She nodded. "As long as you trust Vachon, then I trust that he's sent the best he had."

"I do trust him." He opened the door and motioned her through.

"Then let's get this show on the road." She grabbed his hand and gave it a brief squeeze before she let it go as they walked down the hallway. When they entered the office, a tall dark-haired human turned from where he'd been looking out the window. Xavier was lounging with legs crossed in one of the chairs in front of Duncan's desk but he rose to his feet and faced them as well.

Duncan held out his hand to the other vampire. "Xavier. It's good to see you again."

Xavier shook Duncan's hand. "You as well." He looked at Kimber and tipped his chin in acknowledgment of her presence. "Ms. Treat."

"Please, call me Kimber." See? She could be gracious when it called for it.

Another incline of his head, then he swept an arm out to indicate the man standing by the windows. "This is Hunter McKay, the best necromancer Cleveland has to offer."

As the dark-haired man strode forward, the door opened and Maggie, Brigid, and Atticus entered the room. Leon closed the door, taking his place in front of it, a hulking, silent sentinel.

Introductions were made and hands shaken in greeting. Hunter looked at Kimber and said, "It's a pleasure to finally meet you, Kimber. May I call you Kimber?" At her nod, he went on. "I followed your career before the Outbreak. You had some really difficult cases that you handled with amazing adroitness."

"Thank you." She could read the sincerity in his eyes and knew he wasn't merely trying to butter her buns. "I think I recognize your name, too." She narrowed her eyes, trying to place where she'd heard of him before. "There was something to do with the mayor…"

His grin was a quick flash of white teeth. "Yeah, former mayor Martin Bradley. His Lazarus was just as much a curmudgeon as the old guy had been in life."

"Well, now that the pleasantries are over," Duncan said with a hard glance at Hunter, "let us lay out the plan."

Kimber secretly thrilled to hear the tinge of jealousy in Duncan's voice. Sure Hunter McKay was ruggedly handsome and he had necromancy in common with her, but he had nothing on Duncan. She'd reassure her lover as soon as she could.

Fifteen minutes later, everyone was agreed on the strategy.

Duncan looked toward the back of the room. "Leon, this is where it could get tricky."

"You think?" The big vampire grimaced as he seemed to realize he probably shouldn't have said that out loud. He came closer and waited.

Duncan narrowed his eyes but let that pass. He looked at Atticus. "You and Leon need to organize a squad to go out and bring in two dozen zombies. We'll chain them a little differently than before so that they're in a line to the fence."

"Like a bunch of undead dominoes," Kimber offered with a grin. When no one smiled, she groused good-naturedly, "Tough room."

That got a snort from Hunter and a twitch of the lips from Xavier.

"Is everyone clear on their responsibilities?" Duncan asked.

"Yes, but I object to your involvement," Atticus replied. He turned his silver eyes on Kimber for a long moment, then looked at Duncan once more. "You shouldn't be risking your life. She can use me instead."

Duncan shook his head. "I won't ask it of you, my friend."

"You're not asking. I'm volunteering."

"No." Duncan held up his hand when Atticus began to argue. "The decision's been made. Kimber and I are in this together, all the way." His gaze landed on her.

The love and trust there brought a surge of emotion welling

up in her. She blinked back tears. Now was not the time to fall apart. His life and the well-being of her baby depended on her staying in control.

"How soon can you have things set up?" Duncan asked.

Atticus glanced at Leon and the two of them seemed to share a silent conversation before Atticus said, "Give us six hours. We'll be ready to go a couple of hours before dawn."

Duncan clapped his hands together. "All right, people. That gives us six hours to get mentally prepared and get set up with weapons as well." His glance encompassed everyone in the room. "Good luck to us all."

As the others filed out of the office, Kimber went to Duncan. His arms enclosed her as he held her close. This was how she wanted to prepare herself. She wanted to be wrapped up in his love and support until the only thing she could believe in was that they would not—could not—fail.

Chapter Fourteen

Duncan stood in the courtyard beside Kimber and looked out over the restrained zombies. He bit back a laugh as he remembered her cheeky definition. Undead dominoes, indeed. He hoped they would be, because that would mean the cascading effect they were looking for would happen and this nightmare would end.

Hunter, Maggie, and Brigid should join them any minute now. Natalie and Aodhán stood beside the main doors to the enclave, Aodhán with his long sword clasped in his hand. Natalie looked pale but resolute, and he saw she, too, held her trusty sword. It was about a third the length of the fey warrior's, but Duncan had seen her use it and it was damned effective.

Close to a hundred torches lit the enclosure where he stood as well as the fencing along the front gate, ensuring the area was almost as bright as if they stood in broad daylight. There were eighteen zombies chained in single file, starting at the door to the enclave building straight out to the outer fence where the last one was lashed to the reinforced steel fencing. More zombies had gathered on the outside, drawn by the noise from the clanking of the chains and by the bits of raw meat Atticus and his men had placed on the other side of the fence.

He wrinkled his nose at the strong smell of decomposition. Most of these zombies looked like they'd been riding the apocalypse for months now. He looked more closely at the ones gathered on the other side of the fence and saw a few fresher-looking ones. He didn't suppose it mattered, one way or another. But, damn, cleanup was going to be a bitch.

Leon approached, a grim look on his face. "We may have a problem," he said when he drew near.

What now? "Tell me," Duncan said.

"Some of our people are…resistant."

When he didn't go on, Duncan prompted, "Resistant to what, Leon?"

He glanced at Kimber. "They don't want her to fix this."

"What do you mean?" she asked. "They don't want to stop the apocalypse?" She put up one hand and pinched her nose together, breathing shallowly through her mouth. He guessed the odor of decomp was getting to her.

Leon shook his head. "They think if humans aren't afraid of zombies, they won't be willing donors. That they might, in fact, start targeting vampires, wanting to get rid of us, too."

"There's always been that possibility," Duncan responded. He swept out his arm, indicating the zombies on the other side of the fence, crowding against it, trying to get inside the compound. "But this is no way to live."

"You're telling me," Kimber said. "You'd think they'd want to fix this to get rid of the smell if nothing else."

Duncan couldn't stop his lips from twitching into a small grin. Trust his Kimber to put her finger right on the pulse of things. "We're survivors," he said to Leon. "We'll find a way."

"That's what I told them," Atticus said as he walked up to them, his face dark with a scowl. "Bunch of babies. They've had it easy over the last couple of months, having willing donors right here for the taking, and they don't want to give that up. They've gotten soft. Don't worry. I put the fear of the devil in them." His silver eyes met Duncan's. "There's still time to change your mind. Let me do this for you."

Duncan put a hand on Atticus's shoulder. "I appreciate the offer, old friend. I do. But this is something Kimber and I must do. I can't explain it other than to say I know this in my gut that she and I have to face this together." When his friend's gaze narrowed on Kimber, Duncan added, "And don't even think to threaten her, Atticus. If I end up injured, or worse, it won't be because of Kimber's intention or negligence. Do you understand?"

A muscle flexed in Atticus's jaw. "Yes," he finally said. "But I don't like it. For the record."

"You don't have to like it," Duncan responded. "And, Atticus? If something happens to me, you're my successor. And no action is to be taken against any of the necromancers or Brigid. Understood?"

Atticus gave an abrupt nod, then turned and headed toward the fence where a line of armed vampires stood ready in case the zombies broke through.

Duncan turned to Kimber and drew her into his arms. He rested his forehead against hers and simply held her, feeling her warmth under his hands, her breasts rising and falling with her breaths against his chest. Very soon it would all be over, one way or another. "Whatever happens," he whispered, "know that I love you."

A sighing sob broke from her. "I love you, too, Duncan. So much." She curled her fingers into his back, digging into him through the soft material of his T-shirt. "I don't want anything to happen to you."

"I know you won't let it, sweetheart." He did have faith in her love, in her abilities, but he was also realistic. Sometimes things happened beyond a person's control and you simply did the best you could with what you were given. He wouldn't hold her responsible if things went sideways.

He heard footsteps approaching and looked up to see Maggie, Hunter, and Brigid approaching. "The other necromancers and Brigid are here," he told Kimber.

She pulled away from him and gave a watery smile to her colleagues. Concern on her face, she placed a slender hand on Maggie's shoulder. "Are you sure you want to do this?" She glanced at the woman's protruding belly. "It's not just you we have to worry about."

"It's the same for you, isn't it?" came the tart rejoinder with an equally sharp look at Kimber's midsection. "Did you think word wouldn't get out?" Maggie asked with a smirk.

Kimber heaved a sigh. "No, I suppose not." She looked at Hunter. "You and Maggie need to focus your attention on me, help me tap into the Unseen that's in Duncan. We should only need a little bit to allow Brigid to focus that energy into laserlike precision to blast it into the zombies. Then, boom! Implosion." She swallowed. "I hope."

"It will work," Maggie's voice was as serene as the expression that crossed her face. "I know it will."

Hunter nodded.

"All right, then. Let's do this." Kimber reached for Duncan and squeezed his hand. "Are you ready?"

He leaned down and kissed her on the mouth, pouring all the love he felt for her in that one soft caress. "I'm ready," he said as he straightened.

She blew out a breath. "Here we go."

Maggie stepped closer and grabbed Kimber's other hand, and Hunter slid a hand around the back of her neck. Duncan knew skin on skin was the best way to go, the only way to get the most power quickly, but it rankled to see another man's hand on the woman he loved.

Kimber closed her eyes and inhaled slowly. Her fingers tightened on his hand. He watched as both Maggie's and Hunter's eyes fluttered closed, and Brigid moved forward until she stood between but slightly behind them. She put her hands on Maggie's and Hunter's shoulders and stared straight ahead at Kimber.

Duncan felt the skin on his hand tighten, then flare with prickles of heat that was borderline painful. Another surge and he choked back a yelp that wanted to burst past his teeth. Now that time it *had* hurt.

Her touch grew hot in his. Nerve endings flared, beginning at his hand and traveling up his arm to shoot throughout his body. Searing pain like he'd never felt before made his knees buckle, and he stayed on his feet with effort.

Trying to keep his mind off the agony wracking him, he focused his attention on Kimber. Her pouty lips were drawn into a frown of concentration, and for once, she didn't appear to be in pain. Even as he watched, her face settled into lines of contentment and he realized abruptly that she was taking pleasure in drawing his life force from him.

This time he couldn't stay upright and pain sent him to his knees, hard. Her grip on his hand never loosened. If anything, she tightened her grasp and seemed to draw energy from him even faster. "Kimber," he moaned. He didn't want to stop her; this needed to happen. But he also didn't want her to drain him past the point of no return if it was unnecessary. He was prepared to die to save her life and that of his unborn child, but he wasn't willing to die just so the bit of Eduardo that was woven into the Unseen within her could get his jollies.

Her eyes opened. He stared up at her, his ability to focus coming and going with the waves of agony radiating through him. He saw her irises darken to green just before her pupils dilated, leaving a thin ring of green around them. He could see the struggle taking place as part of her battled to hold on to the newly gained power while the other part, the Kimber he knew and loved, fought to expel it.

"Come on, sweetheart," he urged softly through teeth gritted in pain. "You can do this."

Through the pain, the noises around him seemed to become focused, one after the other. He closed his eyes. There was the constant rattling of chains as the zombies struggled to get free, the murmur of voices, even the chirp of birds in nearby trees. Then a shout dragged his eyes open. The zombie chained to the end nearest the building had managed to break the chain attaching him to the concrete and it now staggered to the side, reaching with skeletal arms, trying to grasp anyone close enough.

With the end of the line loose, the zombies had more freedom to move. In only a few minutes there would be no choice but to start killing them. Duncan watched as Atticus led dozens of vampires to form a row between the shufflers and his small group of necromancers. "Do not let them get through," the Roman vampire ordered.

"Come on, Kimber," Duncan urged.

Her lips drew back in a grimace, and her hand tightened even more on his, mashing his fingers into one another. The bones in his pinkie snapped. A grunt was his only outward concession to the pain. But when his head felt as if someone was driving a spike into it, he couldn't hold back a shout of misery. Through the pain clouding his vision, he saw Atticus turn and start toward him. "Stay where you are," Duncan managed to yell. "Don't break formation. We have to give this time to work."

Atticus's lips thinned but without a word he retook his place. He held his sword at the ready. "Someone get a fire going!" he yelled. "Pass some torches."

Within seconds, flaming lengths of wood were being passed

down the line, and the vampires thrust them toward the zombies, holding them at bay. "This won't work for long," Atticus called out, his face turned to one side. He met Duncan's gaze. "If she's going to do this, now would be the time."

Duncan dropped his chin to his chest and tried to focus on anything other than the agony buffeting him about like a dinghy on storm-tossed seas.

"Now," he heard Kimber say. At least he thought it was Kimber. The voice was deeper than hers, more guttural, the cadence almost that of a man's. Yet instinct told him that was Kimber.

Agony rolled through him. He closed his eyes and fell to one hand, the other still caught up in Kimber's strong grip.

* * *

As Kimber gave her team the go-ahead to push the energy of the Unseen from Duncan to the zombies, she used the Unseen flowing from Duncan to wrap around the dark bit of Unseen that had been squatting inside her all these months and pushed it out of her. She watched the chained shufflers closely for any change and held on to Duncan, though she was throttling back on how much energy she was draining from him. Her breath came fast, part of it from the discomfort caused by the Unseen flowing through her and part of it from equal measures apprehension and excitement.

Maggie and Duncan, on either side of her and standing slightly behind her, both panted lightly, still touching her. Their hands were hot against her skin. Glancing over her shoulder, she saw

Brigid standing tall and slender, her hair flowing behind her as if caught in a wind, her eyes closed, lips moving in a silent chant.

"It's not working," Kimber whispered, dread tightening her throat.

Maggie suddenly gasped, one hand going to her abdomen. "Oh!"

"What is it?" Kimber looked at her, following the other woman's gaze to the ground at her feet. Ground that was wet with the same fluid running down Maggie's legs.

Round eyes met Kimber's. "My water just broke."

Hunter moved and put his arm around Maggie's waist to support her. Both of them were pale.

Kimber wasn't sure how much of that was due to what they'd just gone through and how much of it was the thought of what was shortly to come. Like they had time right now for birthing a baby. "Maggie…"

"I know. I'm sorry." She grimaced. "It's not like I can control this. The baby wants to come out."

Just then Brigid gave a low grunt, drawing Kimber's attention back to her. The fey woman's hands left the shoulders she'd gripped the entire time to press her palms out in the air. "It's done," she rasped, and staggered back.

Kimber let go of Duncan's hand and heard him give a low moan, but her attention was focused on the zombies in chains. If this didn't work, they'd have to figure something else out. Start all over again. She put one hand on her belly. She wasn't sure she had another try in her.

The zombie closest to them stood stock-still, his mouth moving but no sounds emanating from him; then, like a plug being pulled from a socket, all life went out of him and he dropped to the ground. Then the next one dropped, and the next one, and the one after that. All the way to the fence the zombies went to the ground, lifeless.

She stared at the ones on the other side of the fence. Here was the real test. Those in front suddenly stiffened, faces rigid, fingers curled. They fell to the ground. The ones behind them fell. And the ones behind them.

"Oh my God. It's working!" Kimber looked at Duncan and gave a cry. He was lying facedown on the ground, not moving. She dropped to her knees beside him. "Duncan! Are you all right? Oh, God." Fat tears rolled down her cheeks. "I took too much. *I took too much!*"

Atticus knelt beside her and carefully turned Duncan over. Her lover's skin was translucent, his mouth open slightly, eyes closed. With a hard look her way, Atticus lifted his wrist to his mouth and dragged a fang across it, then held it over Duncan's mouth so that blood would drip between his lips.

Kimber hardly breathed, watching for some sign, any sign, that she hadn't killed him. She was vaguely aware of Natalie and Aodhán joining them, swords sheathed as they took up a silent vigil around the vampire who was not only their leader but also their friend.

She heard a moan and glanced up to see Maggie holding on to her abdomen with a pained expression on her face. After several seconds the pregnant woman blew out a breath. "Oh, yeah. This baby is definitely on its way."

Hunter put his arm around her. "I was an EMT back in the day," he said. "Even delivered a couple of babies in the ambulance." He gave Kimber a reassuring look. "We'll take her inside and get her settled comfortably, and I'll make sure she's all right."

"Thank you." Kimber looked back and forth between the two of them. "Both of you, thank you so much. We couldn't have done this without you."

She put her gaze back on Duncan in time to see his tongue come out to swipe at the blood on his lips. Tears rushed down her face. He was going to be all right. He had to be.

"So it did work?" Maggie asked.

Kimber looked toward the fence. She didn't have as good a vantage point from where she knelt beside Duncan, but she couldn't see any zombies milling about. "Oh, I hope so."

"It worked." Brigid's voice was serene. "I can feel the difference already in my magic. Soon the Unseen will be as it was, and all will be right with both our realms."

"After someone does something with all the corpses," Natalie said, wrinkling her nose.

"Come on, gorgeous," Hunter said to Maggie. "We have a baby wanting to be born." He guided her inside, Brigid following closely behind.

"Well, I don't think we can do any good here, either," Aodhán said. "Come, *mo chroí*. Let us go inside and celebrate this victory."

Natalie's face flamed bright red but she giggled and tucked her hand in the crook of his arm and walked away with him.

Kimber stared down at Duncan. Other than that brief swipe of his tongue, he hadn't moved. "Will some of my blood help?" she asked.

"Yes, it will help him heal faster than my blood will."

Without hesitation she said, "Let me borrow your knife."

He drew it from its scabbard and handed it to her. She sliced a furrow across her inner wrist. Bending over him, she placed the wound directly on Duncan's mouth. "Come on, honey," she whispered. "Please. Drink."

His throat moved with his swallow. She stroked the fingers of her other hand along the strong column of his throat, watching it move with his swallows. "That's it. I love you, Duncan. Please don't leave me." Tears slid down her face to drip onto his skin. After a few seconds one of his hands came up and grasped her wrist in a tight hold as his mouth latched on to her wound and began strongly suckling.

Soon enough Atticus removed Duncan's hand from her wrist. Atticus swiped his tongue along her slashed flesh, muttering something about closing the wound, and moved her arm away from Duncan's mouth. "That's enough. He'll be fine."

Duncan's lashes swept up and his green and silver gaze met hers. "Did you do it?"

"*We* did it, I hope."

"And the Unseen in you?" He lifted a hand to cup her face. His fingers trembled against her skin, testament to his current weakness. "Is it gone?"

The serenity that had replaced the swirling aggression inside her was answer enough. "Yes," she said with a smile. "I'm fine.

Now it's time to see to you." She swiped at her tears. "Can you get up? You'll be more comfortable in bed."

His eyes flashed. "If I'm going to be in bed with you, I should be up, shouldn't I?"

"You're going to bed to rest," she said, her cheeks flaring with heat. She shot a glance at Atticus, who met her gaze with steely eyes. She tightened her lips with annoyance and hurt. Sadly this situation hadn't quelled his anger against her, and that was his right. But she missed having him as a friend. She looked at Duncan. "Come on, honey. Let's go up to our suite."

She and Atticus helped him up, each of them sliding a shoulder under his arms to support him as they walked into the building. Though she knew Atticus bore most of Duncan's weight, it still felt good to know she was helping in some way, however small.

* * *

At three o'clock that afternoon, Kimber left Duncan in the bedroom to answer a knock at the door. She swung it open. Atticus stood there. "May I come in?" he asked.

She silently motioned him in. "Duncan's in the bedroom," she said as she closed the door.

"I'd like to talk to you first."

"Oh." She twisted her fingers together, not sure how to proceed. She was tired, too, and unsure of just about everything now. She and Duncan hadn't really begun an intimate relationship until after the Outbreak. If she'd been successful and the zombies really were gone, she wasn't sure where she stood with him after everything that had happened. She'd nearly killed him. How could he not be affected by that?

Of course, she was pregnant with his child. She put one hand on her belly. She didn't want him to stay with her just because she was pregnant. She wanted him to want her for *her*, not because she was having his baby.

Damn pregnancy hormones. Her emotions were all over the place, and she didn't like feeling so unsettled. "What do you want?" she asked, maybe a little more harshly than she'd meant.

He surprised her when instead of glaring at her he shifted his weight as if he were uncomfortable. "A couple of things," he finally said, his gaze on the floor. When he lifted his eyes, she was stunned to see the apology reflected in the silver depths. "I'm sorry for the way I've been treating you lately. I know you didn't attack me on purpose, that what happened was entirely by accident. Perhaps even a happy one, with the way things turned out."

It was more than she'd hoped for. She went to him and wrapped her arms around his waist. He returned the embrace. After a few seconds she pulled back. "Apology accepted."

A ghost of a smile flitted across his lips. "Thank you. Second, I thought you might like an update on Maggie's condition."

"Oh, yes. I've been worrying about her."

Atticus shrugged. "No need to worry. McKay is actually quite good at delivering babies as it turns out. She had a healthy little girl that she named Jacina Kimberly."

There went the water works again. Kimber sniffed. "That's nice," she said, proud when her voice barely quavered.

His cough sounded suspiciously like a cut-off bark of laughter but when she narrowed her eyes at him, his expression was one of solicitous concern. "May I see Duncan now?"

She motioned him into the bedroom. She'd kept a bedside lamp on low so she could watch over Duncan while he slept. He'd awoken only about half an hour ago and had still seemed a little foggy. As he caught sight of Atticus, a smile curled his lips. "How are things?"

"Going well. Maggie had her baby, a girl, but I'll let Kimber fill you in on that. The important thing is this: As soon as the zombies dropped this morning, I sent out several patrols. Some of the first ones have reported back. So far, all of the zombies they've come across are dead. Or dead again." He shook his head. "They're no longer animated, so it appears you and your friends were successful." His voice deepened and he looked at Kimber. "You stopped the apocalypse. Congratulations, and well done."

"I couldn't have done it without Duncan." To have Atticus's respect once again meant more than she could say. "But thank you."

"A few of my patrols went farther afield, so it may be a few days before we hear back from them. But one of the patrols that headed toward Vachon's territory reported back that the squads he sent out are reporting the same thing. No more zombies."

"Thank God." The relief was almost overwhelming. She could have this baby without worrying about flesh eaters.

"Now the hard work really starts," Duncan said.

"Disposing of the bodies and rebuilding civilization." Atticus gave a shrug. "Been there, done that. A plague is a plague, whether it's microscopic or walking around on two legs. Not a problem." With a wink he walked out of the room. In another second she heard the outer door close as he left the suite.

Kimber stood there looking into the empty hallway for several long minutes, feeling bemused and so hopeful she started to feel a little scared. Surely something would come along to ruin the future she could almost see forming before her eyes.

Or maybe she was just a pessimistic scaredy-cat who needed to start seeing the glass half full.

She turned back to the bed and climbed onto it, careful not to jar Duncan. "How do you feel?"

"Same as I did when you asked me half an hour ago," he said with a small grin. "Still a little tired but better than before. I guess twelve hours of sleep will do that for you."

She traced her fingers along his strong jaw. "I love you."

He caught her hand in his and pressed a kiss to her palm, then pressed it to his cheek. "I love you, too, Kimber. And I have a question for you, one that I should have asked months ago." The expression on his face was as solemn as she'd ever seen it. "You make me feel alive in a way I haven't felt since I was human. There is joy in my life where before there was only duty. There is a future to build where before I had only a lonely existence to look forward to." He kissed her palm again. "Marry me, Kimberly Treat."

She wanted to say yes. Oh, how she wanted to. But she

needed to know he wanted her and not just because of the baby. "You're asking me because I'm pregnant?"

A muscle in his jaw ticked. "No, sweetheart." Letting go of her hand, he pulled her down onto his chest and stroked his hand through her hair. "I'm asking because I love you. Because whatever our future holds, I want to face it with you." He lifted his head and pressed his lips to the corner of her mouth in a fleeting, sweet kiss. "Now please put me out of my misery and say yes."

She couldn't stop the grin from spreading over her face. "Yes."

"Yes?" His green eyes seemed to glow as happiness grew.

"Yes!" Kimber pressed kisses all over his face. As he took control, holding her head still so he could dominate her mouth with his, she knew deep down everything was going to be all right. They had each other and in about seven more months they'd have a child. Their child. Maybe they'd have more, and maybe at some point once the children were old enough, Duncan would turn her into a vampire so they could truly have their happily-ever-after. For now she would focus on the present, on the joy they had with each other right now. The future would take care of itself.

Please see the next page for a look
at the first book in the series…

Vampire's Hunger

Chapter One

Kimber Treat, one of only a few necromancers licensed by the county of Summit, Ohio, pushed open the door to the Medical Examiner's lab. "You've got a Lazarus for me?" she asked.

"Yep. Let me get 'im." The Chief M.E. swung open the heavy metal door of the cooler, went inside, and within a few seconds wheeled a sheet-covered corpse into the room. As he did, Kimber took stock of her surroundings. A stenographer perched on a stool nearby, her machine in front of her, fingers poised over the keys. Two burly security guards stood ready, just in case. When the investigation into a murder ran cold and the cops had nothing else to go on, they called in a necromancer.

Most of the time the deceased was revived, questions were asked and answered, and the newly revived was put back to his or her eternal rest. But every once in a while the reaction of the deceased to suddenly being cognizant again was confusion that quickly morphed into frenzied panic. The guards were a necessary precaution.

"You sure you're ready for this?" Homicide detective Carson Bishop moved to stand next to her. He loosened his tie and flicked open the top button of his white shirt, then shoved his fists into the front pockets of his slacks. He tipped his chin toward the sheet-covered body on the metal gurney the Chief M.E. placed in front of her. "Half his face is gone."

She glanced at him then looked at the M.E. "He can talk, though, right? His jaws are intact?"

The older man nodded. "Yep. Most of the damage is to the upper half of his face."

"Then there shouldn't be a problem. Go ahead."

The M.E. folded the sheet down to the collarbones. "Poor fella. This is what taking a gunshot to the face does to ya."

Kimber took a bracing breath before she looked down. Dear God. She'd been around a lot of corpses—with her job there was no way around it—but she'd never seen anything quite this bad. Bile rose in her throat. She swallowed it down and backed up a few steps.

Bishop's hand came out to steady her. "You okay?"

She nodded. She had a job to do, and the sooner she did it the sooner she could get out of there. "I'm fine." She moved forward and rested one hand on the corpse's shoulder. Her palm tingled. Good. Some vitality remained, which let her know this man had been dead only a couple of days at the most. If he'd been dead longer than that, well…With each day that passed after death, the energy dissipated more and more. Then it took a major blood sacrifice—a goat or several chickens—to reunite the soul with the body for even a few minutes. There was awesome power in pain and blood.

But with this poor guy, she could summon his soul by using a relatively small amount, so she'd use her own. Then they could find out who had put him in this state. "What's his name?" she asked.

The M.E. consulted the file in his hand. "Richard Whitcomb."

Kimber wondered who he'd been, what he'd planned to do with his life before someone took it from him. There wouldn't be time to find out. There would only be time to help him through his initial confusion and find out who killed him, if he even knew.

She withdrew the knife she kept sheathed at the small of her back. The hilt was a familiar, comforting weight in her hand. After broadening her stance, she sliced across her inner forearm, a long but not very deep cut, just below a faint row of thin scars. Even though the laceration was shallow, she sucked in her breath at the sharp sting. She walked a circle around the gurney, allowing a miniscule amount of her blood to drip on the floor. Once she'd completed her circuit, she stood inside the circle of power and let her blood drip onto the face of the dead man, making sure it covered his mouth before wiping the blade on the sheet. She slid the knife back into its scabbard. She'd make sure to sterilize it once she got home.

The M.E. handed her a gauze pad and a strip of medical tape. She secured the gauze over her wound and placed her palm on the shoulder of the corpse again. Called by the life essence in her blood, the mists of the netherworld—that shadowy place where all life began and ended—began to stir. So far, so good. Kimber started to chant. "Hear me, Richard Whitcomb. I call you from beyond. I call you to journey from the Unseen to the Seen. By blood and magic I summon you. Arise, Richard. Arise. Come to me now." She always made sure to use the singular when she summoned someone from the dead. She wanted to make sure she was the only one who controlled them. She'd seen firsthand how horrific a summoning could become when the dearly departed had been brought back by someone using "us" and "we" instead of "me" and "I."

She'd never make that mistake again.

The fine hairs on the back of her neck lifted. The magic of the Unseen rippled. The soul was almost reunited with the body. Just one more push should do it. "Richard, come to me. Arise, Richard. Arise!"

The palm of her hand tingled where it rested on his shoulder. He was reanimating. "Just a few more minutes," she murmured.

A surge of power flowed from the corpse up her arm, the energy of the Unseen coursing through her like an electrical charge, making her wince. What the hell? That wasn't normal. She could usually feel the Unseen but it had never reached for her like this before.

Though her instinctive reaction was to shake her hand, she kept it where it was. But she did take a step back, ready to break contact if she needed to, and thereby severing the conduit of her magic with that of the Unseen.

"Everything okay?" Bishop asked. He took a step closer to

the gurney, hand on the gun at his waist, even though she knew that *he* knew bullets wouldn't stop this kind of zombie. Only the one who summoned him, through her magic and force of will, could compel an animated corpse to return to his eternal slumber. He could pump this guy full of bullets and as long as Kimber held sway over him, he'd keep right on coming. Headless, armless, legless, he'd keep on trying until the necromancer returned the essence that animated him to the Unseen.

"Yeah. Yes," she said more forcefully. She had a reputation to uphold. This was a little unusual, but nothing she couldn't handle. She'd been raising the dead ever since her power had manifested when she hit puberty. Almost twenty years now. Granted, eight of those years she'd been under the guidance of a mentor, but still, she had a lot of experience. More than most.

And right now she needed to bear down and put that experience to use. She focused her ability and drew on the Unseen. Another strong wave crashed into her but she maintained her contact with the dead man. "Richard Whitcomb, I summon you by blood and magic. Arise!"

A shudder worked its way through the corpse then pale lids flew open. Or, rather, a pale lid. The eye on the ruined side of his face was gone. Equally pallid lips parted on a groan. His one eye flicked back and forth. Frown lines creased his brow. When Kimber lightly squeezed his shoulder, his gaze skittered to her face.

"It's all right," she soothed. "Richard, you're safe. You can't be hurt anymore."

His mouth worked but no sound came out. His eye widened and he jerked against the metal table.

"Richard, it's all right," Kimber said again. She'd learned long ago that she needed to keep using the deceased's name; otherwise they took a much longer time remembering who they were and what they'd been doing right before they died. "Richard, look at me. Focus on me, Richard."

His head turned and that filmy blue eye fastened on her. His mouth continued to open and close; only now low, gruff grunts came out.

"It's all right," she whispered. "You're safe. Be calm." She felt some of the tension ease from the cold muscle beneath her palm. "That's it." She leaned closer. "Your name is Richard Whitcomb. Do you remember?"

He bobbed his head.

"Good." Kimber was aware on some level of the people around her, but she kept her attention on the dead man. He'd been human, once, maybe he still was, and that meant he deserved her respect. And some dignity. She grabbed the sheet just as it started to slide off to one side, and made sure his nudity remained hidden.

Confusion was still evident in his gaze. She needed to give him time to realize he was dead. Sometimes they got it right away. Sometimes it took a few minutes.

"Wh…where…"

When he didn't go on, she figured he wanted to know where he was. "You're at the County Medical Examiner's office."

His frown deepened. "H…how…"

She tightened her lips. He needed to remember how he got here, not have someone tell him. Otherwise he might not recall the details they were looking for.

"You were shot," the M.E. volunteered.

"Doc," she muttered. She looked at him and shook her head. This wasn't their first dance with the dead. He should know better.

"He seems confused. More than normal," he said. When she merely stared at him, he shrugged. "Sorry."

"Sh…shot?" Richard struggled to sit up. Kimber helped him. When the sheet slid to his waist she gave silent thanks that it kept the important bits covered up. She wasn't a prude, she'd seen naked man parts before, but she wasn't particularly thrilled about seeing them on a dead guy.

"What do you remember?" she asked him.

He gave a slight shake of his head and raised a trembling hand to his face. When he felt the ruin on the right side, he let out a cry.

"Richard, you're okay." Kimber gave another gentle squeeze to his shoulder. "Look at me." She repeated it until he turned his attention to her. "I won't let anyone hurt you again, all right?"

He swallowed. "All right." He looked down at his fingers and clenched them. "Feel…strange."

She couldn't even imagine how weird it was for him. She didn't pretend to know. "Tell me what you remember about that night." She glanced at the stenographer. The woman tipped her chin to acknowledge she was ready.

A low sigh, almost a moan, came from the zombie. "We

fought. We were always fighting. I don't think we knew how to do anything else."

"Who's we, Richard?" Kimber asked.

The click-clack of the steno's keys sounded loud in the otherwise quiet room.

Kimber leaned closer to the zombie. "Who did you fight with?"

He looked up. His confusion and sadness twisted into anger. "She did this to me!" He swung his legs over the side of the gurney. "She killed me."

It wasn't out of the ordinary for a murdered person to be outraged upon realizing what had happened. It also wasn't unusual for them to become physically agitated as a way to work off some of the mental and emotional anguish. Even so, Kimber wanted to keep him as calm as possible. A calm dead man was one who went back to being dead with little effort. "Richard, it's all right. She can't hurt you again."

His one eye held dark rage. "I know she can't hurt me anymore. But I sure as hell can fuck her up."

Bishop took another step forward. "Kimber…"

She waved him off, never taking her gaze off Whitcomb. "Richard, I need you to pay attention." When he ignored her, she lost the soothing tone and made her voice commanding. "Richard Whitcomb, look at me."

He looked at her. She saw something move in his gaze, something that felt dark. Evil. Something she'd never seen or felt before at a reanimation. She tried to ignore the sensation that niggled at the back of her mind, that feeling that something was really, really wrong. She had a job to do; she could manage this.

To re-establish her magical connection, she placed her hand on his shoulder. His skin was still ice cold and dry to the touch. "Richard, who did you fight with? Who shot you?"

"My unfaithful slut of a wife." His thin lips pulled back in a gruesome smile. He jumped down off the gurney.

She tried to ignore the flash of teeth through his ruined cheek as well as the dead man's junk. "We'll make sure she pays for her crime," she promised him. "Now, get back on the gurney and we'll let you rest."

He gave a slow shake of his head. "No. I don't want to rest. And I don't need you to make sure of anything. Oh, no." His chuckle came from a dry throat. "I'll take care of her, don't you worry."

That response wasn't all that unusual, either. The need for revenge was a common theme among murder victims.

Kimber drew upon the Unseen and felt her magic surge within her. "Richard Whitcomb, I command you to lie down."

He stared at her. "No." With a grimace he reached up and gripped her hand. He removed it from his shoulder but held onto it. He looked down at their fingers then began tightening his hand. His head came up and he stared at her from his one eye, malevolent pleasure shining there despite the film of death.

She winced at his hold. "Richard, let go."

"Can you make me, necromancer?"

That was not his voice. Someone—or *something*—else spoke through him.

Bishop moved forward. As he reached for Whitcomb, the

zombie released Kimber and pushed her into the detective. She and Bishop stumbled back. Richard headed for the door.

"Whoa, there!" The M.E. grabbed the zombie by one arm and yanked him to a stop. "You're not goin' anywhere but into the ground, my man."

Whitcomb snarled. He struggled against the doctor's hold, but the older, portly man clearly had some strength beneath the flab. The two security guards and Bishop jumped in, quickly manhandling the zombie onto the gurney. While they held him, the M.E. strapped him in with duct tape while the stenographer looked on.

Every once in a while the woman glanced at Kimber. Her eyes showed her fear and distaste over the situation, as well as a certain amount of distrust. Kimber couldn't blame her—if she'd been at a reanimation and the zombie had run amok, she'd wonder about the necromancer's skills, too.

"Kimber, what the hell?" Bishop faced her, his expression making the craggy lines of his face more pronounced. Rioting emotions enhanced the blue in his usually smoky gray eyes. "What just happened?"

Whitcomb started shouting obscenities and struggling against his bonds of tape. Even though the security guards remained beside him, Kimber kept an eye on him while she answered the detective. "I honestly don't know. There's something more inside him than just his soul."

Whitcomb's single-eyed gaze slid to her. "Wouldn't you like to know what I am, necromancer?" His slow grin sent a shudder through her that she did her best to suppress. He must have seen something, though, because he chuckled. "Not as cool a cucumber as you'd like your friends to think you are, eh?"

"We have what we need," Bishop said. "Finish it."

"She can't!" Whitcomb's shrill laugh bounced off the walls. "Little bitch isn't powerful enough."

"Now, see here…" The M.E. moved closer. "You keep talking like that and I'll duct tape your mouth."

Whitcomb's eyebrows climbed. He looked from the older man to Kimber and back again. "You got it for her bad, don't you, doc? She is awfully juicy, I agree." His gaze shifted to Kimber again. "Bet you're a hot little slut in bed, aren't you, necromancer?" He looked at her breasts and then lingered on the juncture of her thighs. "Yeah, baby. That's one sweet pussy."

"That's it." The M.E. tore off a piece of tape and reached for the dead man's mouth.

Whitcomb lifted his head and sharp teeth snapped down onto the doctor's hand. The M.E. cried out and jerked his hand away to the sound of the zombie's maniacal laughter. Kimber saw the drip of blood before the doctor turned and hurried to the hand wash station.

Kimber put both hands on Whitcomb. Her palms tingled from the supernatural energy animating his body. It surged toward her like before. This time she was prepared and tamped it down with her own magic. She stared into his ruined face and intoned, "Richard Whitcomb, I consign you to the grave. Your soul is released once more to its everlasting journey."

He continued to struggle and curse, but there didn't seem to be as much strength behind his efforts as before.

"Go to your eternal rest, Richard." Kimber ignored the curses he flung her way. She focused all her energy on him and felt the tingling in her hands begin to decrease. It was working. She caught sight of the fresh blood tingeing his mouth and realized she could use that. "By blood and magic, I consign you to eternity."

The fight went out of him like the strings cut to a marionette. Kimber kept her hands on him a few seconds longer, just to be sure. Once she was certain there was no more magic flowing between them, she withdrew her hands and blew out a breath. Now that she was no longer a magical conduit, exhaustion dragged at her. All she wanted to do was go home and climb into bed. She knew, like always, she'd have nightmares after tapping into the Unseen. She just hoped this time they weren't worse than normal.

She looked around the room, meeting the gaze of the other occupants. Forcing gaiety into her voice she said, "Phew! That was something, wasn't it?"

The stenographer stared at her with accusation in her eyes then without a word gathered up her machine and left. The two security guards glanced at each other and followed her out. That left Kimber alone with the M.E., Detective Bishop, and the newly re-deceased Richard Whitcomb.

"That was *not* normal." Bishop's troubled eyes searched hers. "What the hell was that?"

She lifted her hands. "I don't know." At his skeptical expression, she insisted, "Bishop, seriously. I have no idea. I've never had that happen before." She glanced at Whitcomb. "But it's over now, so all's right with the world. He told you who killed him, so…" She looked at Bishop again. "Go get 'er."

He shook his head, but she saw a smile tug at one corner of his mouth. He looked over at the M.E. "Doc? You okay?"

The doctor waved at him without turning around. "I'm fine, though it's the first time I've been bitten by one of my…patients."

It wasn't the first time a zombie had gone after someone like Whitcomb had the M.E., but it was certainly the first time she'd seen one take a bite out of anyone.

"Good. I'll see you later." Bishop looked down at Kimber. "You look tired. This one really took it out of you."

"I'll be all right." He was a nice guy, the real deal. Why she couldn't feel anything romantic for him was beyond her. But then, who had time for romance when there were the dead to raise and put back down? She sent him a smile. "Take care, Bishop."

"You, too. Time to go save the world." He gave her a jaunty two-fingered salute and sauntered out of the room.

Kimber walked over to the M.E. "Are you sure you're okay?" She placed one hand on his upper arm.

He finished taping the gauze wrapped around his hand and held it up. "I'm good to go," he said. He met her eyes. "This is my own damn fault for getting within biting distance. But, hell, girl, none of 'em's ever done that before."

She shook her head. "No, I've never seen it happen, either." And it had never been as hard to put one back to rest. She needed to talk to another necromancer, or maybe a few, and see if they'd ever experienced something like this. Or was she the lucky one?

She made sure Whitcomb was really still dead and said her good-byes to the doctor. She grabbed her handbag from the chair by the door and left the room. As she exited the building, she saw a man sitting on the trunk of her twenty-year-old POS that still ran in spite of being held together by hope and rusted bits of metal. The illumination from the pole light she'd parked under gave a glossy sheen to his black hair. When he saw her he slid to his feet.

Duncan MacDonnough. Vampire prince-wannabe and royal pain in her ass. She'd known him for a couple of years. There'd been an initial, immediate attraction she'd done nothing to fight until the night she'd realized what he was and what that meant for her—that because of him she and her parents had come to the attention of the local vampire queen, and her parents had died.

After that she'd made sure to keep things friendly but not too friendly, but there had always been a sexual undercurrent flowing between them she couldn't deny. She knew if she issued an invitation to her bed he'd take her up on it. She just wasn't overly interested in a relationship where her lover could drain her dry. No matter how sexy he was.

"Duncan," she greeted. After the night she'd had she was in no mood to put up with any of his crap.

"Kimber." His deep, husky voice rasped across her ears. As usual, his demeanor was solemn. Somber. "I hear you had some trouble tonight."

She stopped a few feet away from him and crossed her arms with a scowl. "And how did you hear that?"

"Bishop." He rested a lean hip against the back fender of her vehicle. It creaked and she had the hope it wouldn't fall off. How embarrassing would that be? Duncan added, "We talked briefly when he came out to his car."

She frowned. "What, you've just been hanging out in the parking lot?"

One of his dark brows quirked. On anyone else she would have thought it to be a sign of humor. With Duncan...She didn't think she'd seen him smile more than a handful of times over the years she'd known him. "As a matter of fact...I was not," he said. "I came to see the doc, but when Bishop told me what happened and said you were on your way out, I thought I'd wait to talk to you out here."

"Talk to me about what?"

"You know about what."

She tightened her lips. She was not going to work for him or his queen. There was nothing in the world that would make her join forces with a bunch of bloodsuckers, even if she did regularly spill her own blood on the job. For one, she didn't trust that none of them would bite her. Second, she didn't trust that none of them would bite her. Yeah, that whole biting thing they had going on was the overriding reason she refused to work for them.

She shoved memories of her parents' dying expressions, agonized and fearful, to the back of her mind. "There's nothing to talk about," she muttered and moved forward. "Get off my car."

He straightened and let her unlock the door. As she opened it he said, "Maddalene is very determined, Kimber. And very old, which means she's more powerful than you can know. I've never known her to not get what she wants eventually."

"Well, then, I guess she'll finally have to learn what disappointment feels like." She tossed her purse onto the passenger seat and turned to face Duncan. He was less than six inches away. She gasped and backed up until she bumped into the open car door. She hadn't heard him move. It was surprise that made her move back, that was all. It certainly wasn't because he was a hot, sexy beast that made her want to forget about all her misgivings. It had nothing to do with those clear glass-green eyes of his that seemed to see into her soul. Nothing to do with the way the muscles of his shoulders, arms and chest seemed to beckon her to rest within their shelter. Nothing to do with the way his night-black hair beckoned her fingers to twine in its depths.

He rested a long arm on the roof of her car and bent toward her, effectively caging her in the opening of her car. "Be careful. She won't put up with this attitude of yours any more than she'll continue to accept your refusal." His somber gaze held hers. "She wants your necromancy services, Kimber. She'll keep coming until you give in."

Kimber crossed her arms and tipped her head back so she could look into his handsome face. He had six inches on her in height and outweighed her by at least a hundred pounds, making her feel feminine. Protected, even though he was what he was.

She looked her fill. Pretty, pretty man with long black eyelashes framing those incredible eyes. Her gaze drifted to his mouth, those sensual lips that tempted her so much. She drew in a bracing breath. It would take more than what he had to make her put herself into harm's way. As much as she didn't want to, the memory of her parents' deaths at the hands of vampires—vampires who had been under Maddalene's command—that memory kept flashing into her thoughts. It didn't matter that Duncan had destroyed the ones who'd killed her parents. It was all too little too late. There was no way he would tempt her to forget exactly what he was, what he was capable of.

Yep, keep telling yourself that, Kimber. Maybe at some point it'll actually be true. She cleared her throat. "She can't force me."

"Can't she?" He leaned closer until his mouth was a mere inch from hers. "You have no idea what she's capable of."

"Oh, I think I do. I have a scar to prove it, remember? You were there."

"And you've never forgiven me for not protecting you then."

She clenched her teeth. He'd promised no harm would come to her, and she'd believed him. She'd trusted him. Even after Maddalene had given the order to have Kimber's parents used as vampire bait, Kimber had believed that Duncan would somehow protect her from the bitch queen. He'd kept Maddalene from killing her, but Kimber had a scar that ran from the left side of her throat down her back—a constant reminder of her fight with the vampire race.

"No, I haven't," she said in answer to his claim. In reality, she had, at least intellectually. Emotionally was another matter. It all came down to trust, and she wasn't sure she could trust him.

He was so close she could see herself reflected in his eyes. Her pulse pounded in her throat. She resisted the urge to clap her hand over it, though as close as he was she suspected he could hear the increased rhythm of her heart. She couldn't deny his appeal, and she refused to be ashamed of having a natural reaction of female to male. But she wasn't going to let him seduce her into doing something she didn't want to do. "I said no, and I meant no."

He stared into her eyes. She didn't feel him in her head, so she knew he wasn't trying to use his vampire wiles to influence her. "You need to reconsider," he said, his breath puffing against her lips as he spoke. "I promise you, this time I *will* protect you. With my life if need be." His voice deepened. "I'm telling you this for your own good, Kimber. Reconsider."

She planted her palms on his chest and pushed him back, aware with some anger that the only reason she was able to budge him was because he allowed it, not because she'd been strong enough. "Is that a threat?" she asked, staring hard at him. She didn't care if he was faster and stronger than she was. She wasn't going to let him intimidate her. She made sure her voice was hard and tough. "Are you threatening me?" She almost added "punk" to the end but her sense of self-preservation prevailed.

Nevertheless, his eyes narrowed at her tone. "No, I'm not. I'm trying to help you."

"Help…" She shook her head. Vampires didn't ordinarily go out of their way to help people, especially people like her, people who held sway over the dead. It made them nervous, she supposed, seeing as how they, too, had been dead once upon a time. They had to have the thought, somewhere in the back of their minds, that maybe, just maybe, she'd be able to control them if she put her mind, and her magic, to it. She hadn't ever seriously considered doing it, because if she tried and couldn't, it would be very bad for her. Or if she was successful and then released control—again, it would be very bad for her.

Tapping into the Unseen wasn't something she did on a whim. It took a lot out of her, and she nearly always ended up with nightmares for a few nights after. Most other necromancers she knew did, too. No one really knew why, though they assumed it was because of the power they drew upon to re-animate the dead.

In an effort to sort the mishmash that was her brain at the moment, she closed her eyes for a second. She couldn't think clearly and look into that gorgeous face. When she lifted her lids again it was in time to see his dark head bend close. Passion flared in his eyes before he hid it by dropping his lashes. Then his lips slanted over hers and she lost her breath. And maybe her mind because, God help her, she liked it. A lot.

This was the first time he'd followed through on the desire she'd seen reflected in his eyes from the first time they'd met. A reciprocated desire she kept trying to deny to herself. But now, with his kiss, the truth was impossible to refute. His mouth was cool against hers at first, quickly warming from contact with her lips.

Her eyelids fluttered shut and she leaned into him, wrapping her arms around his waist. Big hands came up and cupped her face, tilting her head to the angle he wanted as he devoured her lips. His tongue glided between her lips to tease and torment. He swallowed her low moan. One hand slid down to her waist, drawing her closer, while the other hand cradled her skull, fingers tangling in her hair.

Kimber slid her hands around to Duncan's back. Feeling off-balance, she gripped his shirt to hold on in a world gone topsy-turvy. The feel of his firm flesh beneath the fabric served to heighten the desire she'd denied earlier. Now it flared to new life, setting her heart to pound hard against her ribs and her core to soften.

He lifted his head and stared into her eyes. Whatever he saw there made him groan. His mouth crashed onto hers again, lips nibbling, rubbing. The hand at her waist moved lower, shaping her buttock, pulling her closer.

The hard evidence of his desire excited her even further. Moaning softly, she pressed against his erection and skimmed her hands up his chest to hold his head. Silky dark hair slid through her fingers.

His mouth left hers to travel along her jaw then down her neck. When his lips slid to the pulse point in her throat, she stiffened and pushed him away. God in heaven, what had she been thinking, letting him kiss her? Letting him get close enough to bite. But that was the problem, wasn't it? She *hadn't* been thinking.

"Kimber—"

"Don't." She held up one hand. "Just…don't." She was tired and felt like an idiot. Another second and she would've let him take her right there against her car. Take her with fangs and cock. She rolled her shoulders and stared at him, feeling like she was a hundred years old. "Anything for your queen, is that it, Duncan?"

He scowled. Apparently he didn't like her calling him a prostitute. Too bad. She didn't appreciate him trying to seduce her so she'd acquiesce to his queen's demands.

"I didn't kiss you because Maddalene wants you to work for her." His face lightened and he looked at her mouth. "I kissed you because I wanted to. Because I've been wanting to taste you, feel those courtesan lips of yours beneath mine."

Now who was calling whom a prostitute? "Did you just call me a whore?" She raised her eyebrows. When he appeared to be a bit discomfited and denied her charge, her good humor returned. She was never one to pass up an opportunity to give a vampire a hard time. "I'm certain that 'courtesan' is a pretty name for 'whore'. And if you think I have courtesan lips, then…" She tilted her head to one side and studied him, pointedly waiting for a response.

"I don't think you're a whore," he finally said. His tone was dry and his expression said *touché* as clearly as if he'd verbalized it. "I do, however, think you're a brat."

She couldn't hold back her grin. It felt good to finally get this composed, always in control man as off kilter as he got her. Even if it was only for a couple of seconds. "I'll see you later," she said and got into her car. She closed the door and cranked down the window. "You can tell your queen that my answer is still no."

As she drove away she glanced in her rearview mirror. Duncan was nowhere to be seen. Sneaky bastard. But what else could she expect? He was a vampire, and they were the definition of duplicitous. It was too bad, really. Now that she'd kissed him, she could definitely go back for more. If he weren't what he was.

For now they'd play this cat and mouse game and she'd see just how long she could hold out against Maddalene Vanderpool's demands.

About the Author

Many writers will tell you they began writing stories the moment they learned to wield a pencil. My own first story was written in sixth grade at the behest of my teacher to write a story with this opening phrase: *It was a dark and stormy night.* But even as a child, I didn't write "kid" stories. I preferred something darker, something that went bump in the night.

As I grew older, I began to read various genres. I especially enjoyed fantasy and science fiction along the lines of J.R.R. Tolkien and Ray Bradbury. I discovered Bram Stoker and Arthur Conan Doyle.

Then I came across romance. Not only could I have fantasy, alien, horror, or mystery, but I could also get a great boy-gets-girl story as well. I was hooked. And along with the passion for reading romance came a passion for writing it as well. After moving to Arizona and working a hectic job for a few years, I joined Romance Writers of America and in 2005 decided to get serious about writing as a career. I was able to take a year off work to focus on my writing. I began with novella-length paranormal stories that I had published with electronic publishers such as Ellora's Cave, Amber Heat, and Liquid Silver Books (under the pen name Sherrill Quinn).

A few years later I sold a werewolf series (also under the name Sherrill Quinn) to Kensington, and in 2012 my Warriors of the Rift series (written as Cynthia Garner) found its home at the Forever imprint of Grand Central Publishing. Most recently I sold a two-part vampire series to Forever Yours, and I hope there are many more to come!

Printed in the USA
CPSIA information can be obtained
at www.ICGtesting.com
JSHW030030030824
67313JS00004B/264

9 781455 552603